MONSTER SWAP

Robbie and Voxy

Written by
JONNY ZUCKER

Illustrated by
TONY ROSS

*Hodder
Children's
Books*

A division of Hachette Children's Books

Hodder Children's Books
A division of Hachette Children's Books
338 Euston Road, London NW1 3BH
An Hachette UK company
www.hachette.co.uk

CONTENTS

After thousands of years spent hidden from human eyes, the earth's monsters have finally revealed themselves. From the murkiest swamps to the deepest forests, the monsters have emerged.

At first, humans were frightened of monsters. After all, seeing a giant purple two-headed monster dribbling mucus through your kitchen window would be enough to put any human off their cornflakes.

And at first, monsters were frightened of humans too. After all, seeing a tiny red-faced toddler human screaming for ice cream would be enough to put any monster off their sour cabbage and soil burgers.

So monsters set up the **MONSTER COUNCIL FOR UNDERSTANDING HUMANS** and humans set up the **Human Agency for Understanding Monsters**. Both organizations agreed that if monsters and humans were to stop being scared of each other they needed to find out as much as they could about each other's lives.

So they arranged a series of exchange visits. These 'Swaps' would involve a human child visiting a monster child in their monster world, followed by that same monster child visiting the human child in *their* world. No one had any idea how these visits would turn out ...

Welcome to the world of

ROBBIE

and the

BOULDER

BATTLE

Dear Voxy and family

Thank you very much for agreeing to host the visit of Robbie Percival, a human boy. As I'm sure you know, Robbie's trip is part of a series of 'Swaps' that are taking place between monster and human children.

I should warn you that Robbie may find some of your Zorb habits strange, and in some cases, disgusting. Please do not worry about this. You will find Robbie's human habits pretty weird too.

For example, humans use bizarre things called 'Knives' and 'Forks' to eat. I mean, who would want to stick a long piece of metal into their mouth when they're trying to eat a frothing bowl of delicious worm soup?

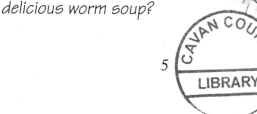

5

And they wear weird things called 'Shoes' on their feet. Everyone knows that going barefoot is far healthier, even if you're walking on hot coals. And if your feet smell cheesy, why not share the stink?

If any of Robbie's behaviour does annoy you, could I please ask you not to bite him?

Wishing you all the best with Robbie's stay.

Yours sincerely

Lady Bug Gazap

'HOLD TIGHT!' shouted the pilot as the plane swooped down.

'WHERE'S THE RUNWAY?' yelled Robbie Percival, looking out of the window and seeing a huge patch of tall spiky red grass below.

'THERE ISN'T ONE!' cried the pilot. 'YOU'RE THE FIRST HUMAN EVER TO COME HERE!'

Robbie couldn't believe it; he was about to meet a REAL monster. He'd been excited about it for weeks, but now he was here! His mind was racing.

What will Voxy look like? What will I do during my visit? Will it be dangerous? And most importantly – what kind of food will the Zorbs eat?

The plane touched down and bumped over the red spikes at great speed until it came to a crunching halt.

Robbie had just unclipped his seat belt when the cockpit door was yanked open and a pair of enormous, paper-thin ears lifted him out of the plane. The ears placed him gently down on the ground. Robbie looked up in amazement at the owner of the ears.

They belonged to a monster who was ten feet tall and three feet wide. His body was covered in light blue fur. He had twinkling dark blue eyes, thick bushy eyebrows with thin, wire-like strands spaced along them, and a brown snout with four nostrils at its base. His two thin arms ended in seven-fingered claws, his two feet were large, puffed up and webbed, and his long tail was flat like a narrow plank of wood.

Robbie felt a mixture of fear and excitement tingle inside him.

'I'm Voxy!' grinned the monster, picking up Robbie's rucksack with his left ear and slinging it over his right ear. 'And you must be Robbie! We're going to have such a great time together! But my dad's cooking supper so we can't be late! COME ON!'

And with that he turned and started running. Robbie raced after him. The red grass came up to Robbie's shoulders and was tickly against his arms. They reached the edge of the field, moving on to a bumpy path that wound upwards. They ran past giant purple trees and through a murky green swamp which smelt of overcooked scrambled eggs. The bubbling and frothing water reached up to Robbie's knees, and when he spotted several pairs of eyes inside it he sped up. In the distance he could see two gigantic pink and white waterfalls and a row of bushes that looked like a line of

massive orange balloons with black spots on.

As Robbie ran, his eyes took in all of the astonishing sights around him.

They'd just started running up a zigzagging yellow path when Voxy called, 'WATCH OUT! PELGO BIRD DROPPINGS!'

Robbie looked up and saw a long-tailed, two-headed dark green bird above. From its backside fell a large lime-green package. Robbie just managed to jump out of its way before the stinky dropping splattered on to the ground.

'Nice move!' laughed Voxy.

At the top of the yellow path, they reached a huge dried-out mud bowl. On its far side, the bowl overlooked a deep valley. Around it stood a series of round circular shacks about thirty feet apart from each other. They were of greenish-brown mud and each one was at least twenty feet tall. Several large dark brown leaves made canopy roofs for the shacks and wisps of curling purple smoke puffed out from some of these.

'This is us!' shouted Voxy, stepping through an archway into one of the shacks. Robbie followed Voxy in and it took him a few seconds to adjust to the dim light. The only things inside were two holes in the ground (one big, one very big) and a small open fire, burning purple logs. The smell of burnt apple pie and vinegar wafted out from the flames. A giant Zorb, with extra-bushy eyebrows, was holding a large black pot over the fire with his snout.

'Hey, Dad!' said Voxy.

'Hi, Voxy!' grinned the big Zorb, turning round. 'AND YOU MUST BE ROBBIE!' He nodded at the small human visitor. 'It's great to have you here! Supper's ready!'

'HOW LOVELY TO MEET YOU!' smiled a slightly smaller Zorb, the tufts of hair on her head wrapped up in some kind of muddy twig curlers. 'I'm Voxy's mum.'

'Hi, Mr and Mrs—' began Robbie.

'Just call us Fru Fru and Weggy,' said Voxy's mum. 'Come on, let's eat!'

Voxy's dad carried the pot to the middle of the shack with his snout and emptied a massive pile of large green and brown spotted discs on to the ground. Voxy and his parents lay down on their sides and started stuffing the discs into their mouths with their ears.

'Sour cabbage and soil burgers – my favourite!' said Voxy, licking his snout.

Robbie gulped nervously.

'Come on and lie down!' said Voxy's dad.

Robbie lay down on his side.

'We don't eat with our claws,' said Voxy's mum, 'but as we don't have any bits of human "cutlery", please feel free to use your hands.'

'Thanks,' said Robbie, breaking off a tiny piece from one of the discs. He popped it into his mouth, expecting it to be absolutely disgusting, but to his surprise it was rather tasty – a bit like cheese on toast.

'Eat loads!' commanded Voxy, munching away like crazy and spitting bits of burger everywhere. 'We need our strength for tomorrow!'

'I take it you're talking about the battle?' said his dad.

Voxy nodded. 'Tomorrow is battle training day, Robbie. And then the two-day Boulder Battle begins!'

'The *Boulder Battle?*' asked Robbie, chewing on a piece of burger.

'Each year we have a battle with the Grobbles – they're the monster clan who live on the opposite side of the valley,' explained Voxy. 'Both clans choose a hundred warriors and then spend two days chucking boulders at each other down on the valley floor. It's brilliant! The clan with the most warriors standing at the end of Day Two gets to rule the valley for the whole year!'

Voxy mimed chucking boulders at Grobble warriors.

'What's the battle about?' asked Robbie.

'It's a tradition,' replied Voxy's mum. 'We've *always* done it. Lots of monsters on both sides don't really want to fight any more, but no one knows how to stop it. Besides, our Warrior Chief, Captain Prush, insists we continue.'

'So does the Grobble Warrior Chief, Captain Mulch,' added Voxy's dad.

'Sorry,' said Robbie in confusion. 'You fight a massive battle and you have *no idea why* you fight it?'

'Who cares what it's about?' butted in Voxy. 'This is the first year I'm old enough to be a warrior! And the great thing is – as my guest, YOU get to be a warrior too!

'Me ... a ... w ... w ... warrior?' spluttered Robbie.

'You don't have to fight if you don't want to,' said Voxy's mum kindly.

'I ... er ... I ... think ...'

16

'EXCELLENT!' cried Voxy. 'I knew you'd be up for it!'

Robbie gulped. *I expected things to be different here, but a boulder battle against an army of Grobbles? That is very, very, VERY different!*

Voxy's dad looked up through the leaf canopy at the quickly darkening sky. 'It's getting late, boys,' he said, shoving the last burger into his mouth, 'you'd better get some sleep.'

Voxy hoovered up all of the burger crumbs from the floor with his snout, and then rolled on to his stomach and used his tail to start drilling a third hole in the ground. He worked very quickly.

'This,' he declared, when he'd finished, 'is your very own mud bed!'

He pulled one of the leaves off the roof and threw it to Robbie. 'And that's your blanket – for a perfect night's sleep!'

Robbie looked down into the hole. *A perfect night's sleep? I don't think so!*

Voxy's mum and dad climbed into the extra

big bed, Voxy lowered himself into his one, and Robbie hesitantly lay down in his. He rolled up his jacket for a pillow and covered himself with the leaf. He twisted and turned until he found a semi-comfortable position. It took him a while to get to sleep, partly because Voxy and his parents had fallen asleep instantly and were snoring like thunderstorms, and partly because his brain was fizzing.

When I first saw Voxy I was a bit scared of him. After all, he is gigantic! But he's really friendly so I reckon we're going to be great mates. And the Zorb settlement is cool – apart from the Pelgo bird droppings! But the Boulder Battle is another matter. I'm going to be a warrior! I'm absolutely tiny compared to all of the monsters here. Is there any way I'll get out of the battle alive?

After a breakfast of earwig flakes in slug juice (which tasted a bit like spaghetti and meatballs, but crunchier) Robbie and Voxy hurried down a long, wide path. Every few steps, they were joined by other Zorbs.

'All of our warriors,' explained Voxy.

Some of the Zorb warriors were the same age as Robbie and Voxy, some were a few years older, but most were adults, and the majority were way bigger than Voxy. Robbie had seemed small last night, but now he felt like an ant.

Several of the Zorbs called out greetings to

Robbie, like 'Hi there, human boy!' and 'Great to have you in our army, kid!'

Robbie gulped. *What have I let myself in for?*

The path led to a walled courtyard made from large, jagged pink stones, and it wasn't long before all ninety-nine Zorb warriors had gathered, with Robbie as the hundredth fighter.

'I can't wait to get out there tomorrow!' said Voxy, flicking his ears left and right. 'Just bring on those Grobbles!'

A moment later, all talking in the courtyard suddenly stopped. A huge and ferocious-looking Zorb with a green eye-patch had just appeared.

'That's Captain Prush,' whispered Voxy.

The Captain stood for a moment, looking round at his warriors. His eyes came to a stop when they fixed on Robbie.

'You must be our human visitor,' he said in a low growl.

Robbie nodded his head nervously.

'Can I trust you?' demanded Prush.

'Er ... I think so,' replied Robbie.

'He's going to be ultra brave and awesome on the battlefield!' called out Voxy.

'We'll see about that!' barked the Captain.

Voxy was about to say something else, but Prush gave him such a scowl that he remained silent.

'Right!' boomed Prush. 'We will begin our training with target practice.'

A team of Zorbs began sticking life-size pictures of Grobbles all round the walls of the courtyard. Each Zorb warrior had their own Grobble poster to aim at.

The Grobbles were a bit shorter than the Zorbs, but still enormous compared to Robbie; they had tall pointy heads, bright red skin, razor-sharp teeth and thick black arms with chunky fists.

Robbie looked at the pictures with a knot of fear in his belly.

Talk about a scary enemy!

Large baskets of boulders were then passed around. Robbie pulled out three. They were light brown, about three times the size of a tennis ball and had very tough leathery surfaces.

'ATTACK BEGIN!' yelled Captain Prush.

Robbie pulled his arm back and threw a boulder. It landed way short of his target. He chucked another, but this one landed even further away. Cricket wasn't really his sport so he hadn't had much practice hitting targets.

All around him, Zorbs were chucking boulders at their Grobble posters and each hit made a huge thudding sound.

This isn't just some game they're preparing for, it's a real battle! If one of those boulders clonks me on the head, I'll be out for weeks!

But even though everyone was trying their best, Robbie could see from many of the Zorbs' faces that their hearts weren't really in it. He remembered Voxy's mum's words:

Lots of monsters on both sides don't really want to fight any more, but no one knows how to stop it.

'You must know *something* about how the battle started,' he said to Voxy, who was standing a few feet away, preparing to throw four boulders at his Grobble poster – two with each ear.

'You heard – it's a tradition,' replied Voxy. 'It's as simple as that. Now can I get on with hitting my Grobble?'

Robbie spent the next forty minutes trying to hit his poster. He threw under-arm and over-arm, sideways and frontways, high shots and low shots. But he still got nowhere near.

'THAT'S ENOUGH!' shouted Captain Prush, walking round the courtyard and seeing how many hit marks there were on each warrior's Grobble poster. When he came to Robbie's poster he looked at it and frowned at the lack of any hit marks.

'Ultra brave and awesome,' he said with a sneer, 'I don't think so!'

'He tried his best!' cried Voxy. 'You've got to give him a chance!'

'THERE'S NOT ENOUGH TIME FOR TRYING!' barked Prush. 'I NEED INSTANT RESULTS! We now move on to defence.'

Small metal shields were handed out to each Zorb warrior. Robbie looked at the shield he was given in amazement. It was small with a thin clunky handle.

This thing couldn't protect a sour cabbage and soil burger, let alone a Zorb!

The Captain faced his troops and suddenly, without warning, began hurling boulders at everyone; with his ears, his tail, his snout and his eyebrows. Boulders zinged around the courtyard. Robbie dived and leapt to avoid the flying boulders. He got the feeling that Captain Prush was aiming more boulders at him than at any of the other warriors and he was relieved to be hit just once, a glancing and not very painful blow on the ankle.

When the defence session ended, Robbie put up his hand.

'Yes, human boy?' said Prush.

'I think I could design you a better battle shield,' said Robbie.

'WHAT?' snapped the Captain.

'The shields,' said Robbie, 'they're a bit small.'

Prush completely ignored Robbie and called out, 'MATRON BAB!'

A huge female Zorb strode into the courtyard. Her ears were tied back and pinned to her fur she had a large badge stating:

DO WHAT THE MATRON SAYS OR GET WHACKED!

'Many of you will be injured in battle,' said Captain Prush, eyeing his troops. 'Matron will be running our field hospital. If you do get hurt you will obey her every command!'

'There is no way I am going to get injured and end up in *her* hospital,' whispered Voxy. 'She's the toughest Zorb around.'

Robbie shivered as Matron Bab swept out of the courtyard.

'And now,' announced Captain Prush, 'it is time for this year's secret weapon.'

There were excited whispers all around.

He clapped his hands and two long-haired Zorbs wearing backwards-facing tiny baseball caps entered the courtyard, dragging a large green, cannon-like machine on wheels.

'That's Frazzle and Spit,' said Voxy. 'They're our techno crew – they invent all of our battle gear.'

'Slow down, dude!' puffed Frazzle.

'No way!' replied Spit. 'We're, like, way behind schedule!'

They stopped when they reached Captain Prush's side.

'Last year,' said Prush, 'the Grobbles used mini trampolines to gain height advantage over us, and that helped them win that battle. This year we will get our revenge. Let me introduce you to the Zorb Flinger – designed and built by Frazzle and Spit. The Flinger fires one brave warrior high into the air, from where they can pelt the enemy with boulders. Who will volunteer to try it out?'

28

Robbie's hand shot into the air. *I'll show him how brave I am!*

The Captain narrowed his eyes.

'Er, maybe it would be better if I did it,' piped up Voxy. 'After all the Flinger *is* designed for a Zorb.'

'No,' said Robbie firmly, 'I WANT to do it!'

'I seriously doubt if I can trust you, human boy,' tutted the Captain, 'but I'll give you a chance. Enter the Flinger and let's see what you're made of.'

Voxy put a paw on Robbie's shoulder to try and make him change his mind, but Robbie brushed it off and mouthed, *'I'll be OK.'*

With his heart beating ferociously quickly, Robbie walked across the courtyard and climbed feet-first into the Flinger's mouth. Beads of sweat spread across his body. Nerves jangled inside him. Captain Prush nodded and Spit pressed the large red **FIRE** button on top of the machine. There was a tremendous

as the Flinger exploded into life.

But instead of shooting Robbie straight up into the air, the Flinger shot him over the courtyard wall, across the mountain top, and down, down, down, into the deep valley below.

'AAAARRRGGGHHHH!' yelled Robbie as he zoomed down towards the valley floor.

Forget scrambled eggs – I'm going to be scrambled human!

WHOOOOOSH!

went Voxy's tail as it shot over the wall. It found Voxy's new human friend with its tail sensor, scooped Robbie up and lifted him with a crash back into the courtyard.

The watching Zorbs trumpeted through their snouts to applaud Voxy's amazing rescue.

'I knew I couldn't trust you!' shouted Captain Prush at Robbie.

'It wasn't his fault!' cried Voxy. 'He was brave just to volunteer, let alone be fired from that thing! It's the Flinger you can't trust!'

'SILENCE!' barked Prush.

'Are you OK?' asked Voxy, looking anxiously at Robbie.

'I think so,' replied Robbie, feeling shaky, but happy not to be scrambled.

I wish all of my other friends had tails like that!

Prush turned to Frazzle and Spit. 'As for you two TECHNO-IDIOTS, the Flinger MUST be working properly in time for the battle tomorrow! DO YOU GET ME?'

'No problemo, dude,' replied Frazzle.

'Like ... absolutely,' nodded Spit.

They immediately started arguing with each other about whose fault it was that the

33

Flinger had misfired.

'Right,' said Prush, swivelling back to face his troops. 'We will meet again at night fall. Until then, you are all dismissed.'

The Zorb warriors started moving out of the courtyard through one door, but Voxy grabbed a boulder basket and pulled Robbie through another door. 'Let's get in some extra practice,' he said.

They headed up a sloping path, leaping over some steaming, furry, brown rock-pools, and swerving to avoid another falling lime-green parcel from a two-headed Pelgo bird. They stopped inside a ring of the large purple trees.

'OK,' said Voxy, making a large circular mark on one of the trees, with his tail. 'Let's throw some boulders.'

While Voxy's shots kept hitting the mark, Robbie couldn't get the boulders anywhere near it. But he kept on trying, with throw after throw after throw, until a couple of hours later, he finally started getting close. A short while after that, he finally hit the target.

'EXCELLENT!' beamed Voxy. 'You'll show Captain Prush!'

They took a break, sitting with their backs against the marked purple tree, eating the Bark and Bones sandwiches Voxy had brought along. Robbie didn't ask who the bones belonged to. The sandwiches tasted a bit like cornflakes mixed with paper. He didn't complain, but he *did* wish he'd brought along some of the Jelly and Mango crisps he'd made at home a couple of weeks ago.

'Why does Captain Prush hate me so much?' Robbie asked between mouthfuls.

'He's like that with everyone,' replied Voxy.

'It felt like he dislikes *all humans*.'

'Do you think so?' asked Voxy. 'I'm not so sure.'

'And another thing,' went on Robbie. 'Why

do you use *boulders* to fight? Why not stones or chunks of wood?'

'I haven't got a clue,' replied Voxy, 'but there are ten sandwiches left. Do you want any of them?'

Robbie shook his head and let Voxy polish them off.

After their break, they carried on practising. Robbie began hitting the target more often and gained quite a bit more confidence, although it still didn't stop him worrying.

My aim might be getting better, but if any of these boulders hits me hard, it's going to seriously hurt!

They stopped at night fall when Captain Prush's call rang out through the settlement. They headed across a bumpy blue field. In the distance to their right were two buildings, about fifty feet apart from each other. The first looked like a tall mud-baked pancake, and the second was a tin hut.

'What are those?' asked Robbie.

'The big one's my school,' replied Voxy.

'Do you do reading and writing and boring stuff like that all day?' asked Robbie.

Voxy shook his head. 'Zorbs used to be able to read and write but that was ages ago. Now only Captain Prush and a few of the elders can, and even they can't do it very well.'

'So what *do* you do all day?' asked Robbie.

'We play Melafon,' grinned Voxy. 'It's a brilliant Zorb game.'

Playing a game all day instead of having lessons? Zorbs are so lucky!

'What about the smaller building?' asked Robbie.

'That's the Junk Store. It's where we keep all of the stuff we don't need any more. It's falling to pieces and is strictly out of bounds.'

They walked on and a few minutes later they reached a clearing. Frazzle and Spit were tying some sort of huge green candles to tree branches. Zorb warriors were lying on their sides, talking about tomorrow's battle. When Captain Prush marched into the clearing everyone fell silent.

'It is time for the Zorb battle chant and dance!' he declared.

In a moment everyone was on their feet.

'MOO!' chanted Prush.

'MAH!' chanted his warriors.

'MAH!' cried Prush.

'MOO!' the troops shouted back.

The chant got louder and louder, the Zorbs stomping round the clearing, bumping bellies with each other. Robbie got caught up in the atmosphere and soon he was chanting as loudly as everyone else. But when he bumped bellies with Voxy, he was sent flying backwards into a tree. As he picked himself up he heard another battle chant, carried on a gust of wind across the valley. His stomach lurched.

The Grobbles! he thought, a shiver zipping down his spine. *Tomorrow I'll be fighting them! I'll be the smallest warrior in the valley by far! Can I really go through with this?*

'BE SEATED!' ordered Prush. Everyone lay down again.

'It is now time for the traditional pre-battle spying mission into the enemy camp,' said Prush

quietly, his eyes scanning the Zorb faces in the
light given off by the green candles.

'And this year, I would like the two spies to
be ... Voxy and his human friend. Let us see if I
can trust a human with something so important!'

There he goes again! What has he got against me and the rest of the human race?

'Well, what are you waiting for?' asked Prush, staring at Voxy and Robbie. 'The time to strike is NOW!'

4

'I *have* to show Prush he can trust humans,' said Robbie as he and Voxy crept down the Zorb mountain into the valley.

'We'll get so much enemy info he won't know what's hit him!' replied Voxy.

They reached the valley floor and stole past several huge thickets of bare, knobbly trees, over a dried-out lake and round some large clumps of high, hissing thistles. As they started to climb the Grobbles' mountain, Robbie's body tensed up. They neared the top and crouched down behind a large, spiky

bush, raising their heads a little to take a peek.

The Grobble settlement was surrounded by a high wall made from some kind of thick and winding brown plant. There was only one way in, through a high gate, but this was guarded by three very fierce-looking Grobble guards. They looked exactly like the posters in the courtyard, their tall pointy heads and bright red skin gleaming in the moonlight.

'How are we going to get past that lot?' whispered Voxy.

They were both silent for a while, but then Robbie suddenly had a brainwave. He pulled his dad's old mobile phone out of his pocket. You couldn't make calls on it but its games and music worked fine.

Robbie flicked the phone on and selected the loudest track on its playlist – *Mash Up* by Anvilla Egghead and the Gazelles of Death.

'What are you doing?' hissed Voxy.

Robbie pressed PLAY and lobbed the phone

into another bush about twenty feet away. Ear-busting heavy metal guitar chords spilled out of the phone's tiny speaker, along with the hoarse screams of Anvilla Egghead.

Mash up!
Mash up!
We're gonna have
A smash up!

The Grobble guards immediately rushed to the bush and dived inside it, yelling, 'SHOW US YOUR PAPERS OR WE WILL EAT YOU!'

'Go!' hissed Robbie.

He and Voxy jumped out from behind their bush and raced through the gate.

They ran along a bumpy path, surrounded on each side by shops made out of what looked like black broccoli, and jumped over a large puddle of gooey, silver oil. When they heard some Grobble warriors approaching – arguing

45

about who would hit most Zorbs tomorrow – they dived behind a mound of jagged stones until the warriors had passed.

'Hey, listen!' said Robbie.

Nearby the dull sound of thwacking cut through the night air.

'It's coming from over there,' said Voxy, turning left. They tiptoed down a narrow passage, drips of a cheesy-smelling liquid plopping on to their heads. Robbie brushed the drips away, and Voxy ate them. They stopped at the end of the passage and peered round.

A ferocious-looking Grobble wearing a large tin helmet was standing in a square space, talking to a large group of Grobbles, whose eyes were all locked on to him.

'That's Captain Mulch,' whispered Voxy in awe. 'He's ultra tough and ultra mean!'

'And now, for this year's top-secret Grobble weapon!' announced Mulch.

46

Robbie and Voxy looked at each other with big eyes.

Two Grobble warriors brought out a large, upright metal tube with a big hole on its front side.

'Say hello to the Grobble Pounder!' said Captain Mulch proudly, turning the contraption to face his troops. He tipped ten boulders into the top of the tube and flicked a lever on its side. Instantly, the ten boulders shot out of the hole at fantastic speed, flying straight at the group of watching Grobble warriors. They had to dive for cover to avoid being hit.

'Come on,' urged Voxy. 'We've seen it; now let's get out of here!'

'Just a minute,' whispered Robbie. 'I want to see how it works!'

'Are you CRAZY?' hissed Voxy.

Unfortunately, he said this a bit too loud. Captain Mulch and all of the Grobble warriors spun round and spotted the two faces peeping out from the passage.

'SPIES!' yelled Mulch. 'A ZORB WARRIOR AND AN UNIDENTIFIED FREAKISH CREATURE!'

'Maybe you were right about leaving now,' said Robbie.

'GET THEM!'

yelled Captain Mulch.

B ack down the narrow passage Voxy and Robbie flew.

If they catch us neither of us will get a chance to throw a single boulder! We'll be Grobble mincemeat!

The front gate of the Grobble settlement was now in sight. The three Grobble guards were standing by the gate, their backs to Robbie and Voxy. They were covering their ears and wildly pushing buttons on Robbie's phone in an attempt to stop the wailing and thrashing of Anvilla Egghead and the Gazelles of Death.

Mash up!
Mash up!
We're gonna have
A smash up!

The guards turned round when they heard Robbie and Voxy's thundering footsteps.

'PRODUCE YOUR PAPERS OR WE WILL EAT YOU!' they shouted.

But Voxy was ready for them. He shot out his tail and whacked all three of them in the chest. They screamed and went crashing to the ground. The one holding the phone let go of it. It flew through the air and Robbie caught it as he and Voxy jumped over the guards' bodies.

A second later, Voxy and Robbie were through the gate and running for their lives.

The Grobble guards tried to stand up but were pushed back down by Captain Mulch and his angry gang of Grobble warriors.

'STOP THE SPIES!' yelled Mulch.

Robbie and Voxy raced down the Grobble
mountain into the dark valley. Robbie took a
quick look round and saw the chasing warriors
thundering after them.

'FASTER!' he yelled at Voxy.

They hit the valley floor with the Grobbles
gaining on them by the second.

'We're never going to make it!' shouted
Voxy.

But an idea suddenly popped into Robbie's

brain. 'Quick, this way!' he shouted, grabbing his monster mate by the ears and leaping straight into a huge clump of hissing thistles.

'OUCH!' cried Voxy as they landed in the middle of the clump, picking up loads of scratches on their way.

'SHHH!' commanded Robbie, pulling his shirt sleeves down to protect his hands, then frantically grabbing great handfuls of thistles and knotting them together in a tepee-like structure above their heads.

'This is the most uncomfortable hiding place EVER!' moaned Voxy.

'THEY MUST BE HERE SOMEWHERE!' shouted Captain Mulch on reaching the valley floor. 'AND WE WILL NOT LEAVE THE VALLEY WITHOUT THEM!'

Robbie and Voxy squashed their bodies as far down as possible and held their breath.

For a few minutes it seemed like the Grobbles wouldn't come anywhere near them, but then a large and snorting one strode over and knelt down by their thistle clump. He picked up something that was caught on one of the loose thistle spikes. It was a small piece of Robbie's shirt that had been torn off.

The Grobble started dribbling with excitement. 'I know you're in there!' he cooed, starting to untie the thistles. Robbie closed his eyes in terror.

Please don't chew when you eat me! Just swallow me down in one go!

The horrible noise of more thistles being untied sounded above them.

'Nearly there!' laughed the Grobble.

But just as he was about to untangle the last few thistles, Captain Mulch's voice called out. 'NOT OVER THERE! WE NEED YOU HERE!'

'But I think I've—' protested the Grobble.

'NO!' shouted Mulch. 'OVER HERE NOW!'

The Grobble reluctantly let go of the thistles and hurried away in Mulch's direction. Robbie and Voxy didn't move a muscle for a good five minutes and when they did they let out the longest sighs of relief. The Grobbles were now searching for them at least fifty feet away, with Captain Mulch's angry voice getting more and more distant. Moving with as little sound as possible, they quickly began running up the Zorb mountain.

They reached the top and sprinted with excitement to tell Captain Prush of their discovery.

Now he'll pay me some respect! thought Robbie.

They found the Captain sitting in the clearing. A short distance away Frazzle and Spit were making last-minute changes to the Flinger. Frazzle's head was inside the barrel while his lower half jutted out.

'Twist that red dial, dude!' his echoey voice commanded.

'I'm, like, doing it,' replied Spit.

Prush looked up when Robbie and Voxy approached.

'Well?' he demanded.

'The mission was a great success,' said Voxy.

'We found out what the Grobbles' secret weapon is,' added Robbie proudly.

'Show it to me!' ordered Prush.

Robbie and Voxy looked at each other. 'Er, we haven't actually *got* it,' said Voxy, 'but we saw it and we know—'

'SILENCE!' shouted Prush.

At that second there was a whizzing sound and instead of being fired out of the Flinger, Frazzle's whole body was dragged inside it.

'Not good, dude,' echoed his voice.

'Unless you have the weapon in your hands, your mission has failed!' snarled Prush.

'But ... but ...' tried Voxy.

'NO!' snarled Prush. 'YOU ARE DISMISSED.'

He turned his back on them.

Robbie and Voxy walked slowly away from the clearing, their hearts heavy, their spirits low. Their excitement of a few moments ago had completely vanished and now they both had the feeling that they'd let down the entire Zorb monster clan.

'Can you bang in those nails?'

It was early the next morning. Robbie and Voxy were kneeling outside Voxy's shack. There were scraps of metal lying on the ground all around them. They'd only been up an hour, but Voxy's parents had already warned them about ten times to be extra careful on the battlefield.

'We want you both back in one piece!' said Voxy's mum.

'Keep your wits about you at all times!' added Voxy's dad.

Voxy lifted his tail and hammered the last few nails into the two brand new shields Robbie had designed late last night. The shields had a far bigger defending area than the traditional Zorb ones and were easier to hold, with two metal loops to put your paw/ear/tail through.

'I can't believe we've been using those rubbish Zorb ones for all these years!' cried Voxy, picking up one of the new shields with his ears and swinging it round above his head to bat away imaginary boulders thrown by imaginary Grobbles.

'They're not bad, are they?' said Robbie modestly.

'Captain Prush is going to love them!' shouted Voxy.

*

'I HATE THEM!' declared Captain Prush. 'I LOATHE THEM, I DESPISE THEM, I DETEST THEM!'

All of the Zorb warriors, including Robbie and Voxy, were lined up in neat rows in the courtyard. Robbie had left the two new shields on the ground at the front for the Captain to inspect.

'But Captain Prush,' said Voxy, 'they're *way* better than the old shields. They have a bigger defending area, they have a—'

'SILENCE!' bawled the Captain. He walked over to where Robbie and Voxy were standing and leaned so far down that they could feel his hot, salty breath on their cheeks.

'The Zorb clan have always used the traditional Zorb shield for the two-day Boulder Battle!' growled Prush. 'My father used it; my grandfather used it; my great-grandfather's third cousin's son used it. It was good enough for them, so it's good enough for me! Do you get my meaning?'

Robbie and Voxy nodded glumly.

'If you want to take those ridiculous new

shields on to the battle field then so be it,' said Prush, 'but don't come crying to me when they let you down!'

Robbie sighed with disappointment. *There is no pleasing Captain Prush!*

'Right!' boomed the Captain's voice, 'battle hour is almost upon us. We must move!'

Robbie found himself caught up in the great mass of Zorbs pouring out of the courtyard. 'Stick close to me,' said Voxy.

Prush marched them out of the courtyard, along the wide path and across the huge mud bowl. Voxy's parents and lots of other Zorbs watched them pass, smiling and waving and wishing them good luck. Prush and his warriors stopped when they reached the tip of the mountain. A few seconds later the Grobble army appeared on the tip of *their* mountain. An eerie silence settled in the valley as the two sets of warriors gazed out at each other. Robbie felt the tension cranking up all around him as his nerves went crazy. *Who's going to win the first day's battle, and how badly will I get hurt?*

Somewhere in the distance a bird squawked the hour.

Captain Prush looked at his troops and barked one word: 'CHARGE!'

The sight and sound of the two monster clans crashing down into the valley was quite spectacular. Their roars and screams exploded into the morning, their faces twisted in fear, excitement and determination. Robbie charged down with everyone else, his new shield strapped on to his left arm, two boulders in each hand. Frazzle and Spit were just behind him; Frazzle pulling a gigantic crate of boulders, Spit pushing the Zorb Flinger.

As soon as the warriors reached the valley floor, the battle began. Boulders flew in all directions. Wherever you looked, snouts, paws and ears were all hard at work.

Almost immediately, Robbie had to dive

on to the ground to avoid being clonked on the head by a low-flying Grobble boulder. He chucked his first boulder and watched with disappointment as it was easily batted away by a chunky Grobble claw.

Voxy was right beside him, hurling boulders with both ears, whooping with delight and leaping out of the way when enemy missiles headed towards him. Captain Prush was a short distance away, batting boulders at the Grobbles with quick movements of his tail.

It wasn't long before warriors on both sides took big hits and crashed on to the ground. A giant scoreboard had been set up in the middle of the valley floor. After the first hour of battle, it read:

ZORBS: 9 warriors down
91 still standing
GROBBLES: 4 warriors down
96 still standing

Robbie frowned and threw another boulder. It missed a Grobble by a fraction.

As the battle raged on, more and more warriors on both sides were struck down and helped off the battlefield.

No wonder so many of them don't want to fight any more, thought Robbie.

A little while later, Robbie spied a group of Grobbles pushing some trampolines to their front line. Grobble warriors then started taking turns to bounce up on the trampolines and pelt the enemy with boulders.

'BRING ON THE FLINGER!' shouted Captain Prush.

Frazzle and Spit wove through the throng of battling Zorbs, dragging the Flinger to Prush.

'Dude, let's do this thing,' said Frazzle.

'Like, yeah!' replied Spit, jumping inside the barrel, a huge pile of boulders clasped in his hands. Frazzle quickly pressed the red **FIRE** button.

But instead of being shot upwards, Spit was fired round and round in circles like a balloon that's just been popped.

‘NOOOOOOOOOOO!’

shrieked Captain Prush at the top of his voice.

'What happened, dude?' shouted Frazzle, rushing over to Spit, who had crashed on to the ground.

'I, don't, like, know,' replied Spit, rubbing his head.

'YOU IDIOTS!' yelled Captain Prush.

Robbie quickly checked the scoreboard.

ZORBS: 26 warriors down
               74 still standing
GROBBLES: 12 warriors down
               82 still standing

66

It's really not looking good!

'I'll be back in a minute!' he shouted at Voxy, dodging a few low-flying boulders and running over to the Flinger. Captain Prush was busy screaming at Frazzle and Spit, so none of them noticed Robbie's arrival. He flipped open a panel at the back of the machine and quickly switched some wires around. He then twisted a couple of dials on the underside of the Flinger.

Just as he was finishing up, out of the corner of his eye, he saw that Spit had turned round and was watching him with a raised eyebrow.

Robbie ran back over to Voxy and grabbed a couple of boulders. Just before he threw them he took a quick look round and saw Spit whisper something in Frazzle's ear. Immediately they raced to the Flinger. Frazzle jumped in and Spit pressed the FIRE button. With a great whooshing sound, Frazzle was fired high into the air, where he showered a group of Grobbles with a fistful of stones.

'AT LAST!' roared Captain Prush triumphantly. 'I KNEW YOU TWO COULD DO IT!'

The fighting went on right through the morning:

ZORBS: 39 warriors down
61 still standing
GROBBLES: 32 warriors down
68 still standing

And deep into the afternoon:

ZORBS: 50 warriors down
                50 still standing
GROBBLES: 46 warriors down
                54 still standing

The battling warriors on both sides were getting more and more tired.

I can't believe they carry on with this battle, year in, year out, when they don't even know what it's about! If only I could find out, I might be able to stop it! thought Robbie.

A short while later a boulder struck Robbie's elbow. The pain wasn't too bad and he carried on, making a great strike on a Grobble's knee which forced the Grobble to leave the battlefield.

Yes!

It was getting dark when Robbie checked the scoreboard again:

ZORBS:	58 warriors down
	42 still standing
GROBBLES:	58 warriors down
	42 still standing

We've caught up with them!

At that second he spotted three Grobbles wheeling out the Grobble Pounder and loading it up with ten boulders. They aimed the Pounder directly at Captain Prush and fired.

'DUCK, CAPTAIN PRUSH!' yelled Robbie as ten boulders hurtled straight towards his head.

But Prush didn't hear him.

Robbie pulled off his new shield and hurled it frisbee style through the air. It flew into the path of the ten boulders and whacked them all on to the ground. But the shield flew on and bashed straight into Captain Prush's back. Frazzle had seen the whole episode and rushed to tell Prush what had happened, but Prush waved him away and just stood there, scowling furiously at Robbie.

And then a loud cry of pain rang out. Robbie spun round and gasped in horror.

Voxy had taken a direct hit.

He was lying on the ground, with a huge hole in his left ear.

Robbie rushed over and knelt down at his monster friend's side. The fur around his ear hole was glowing with an orange pulse.

Poor Voxy! That looks terrible! Will he ever be able to get his ear repaired?

'It's nothing,' said Voxy bravely.

'Medical dudes coming through!' shouted Frazzle as he and Spit swerved round several boulder-throwing Zorbs, carrying a stretcher – which was very badly made from long branches and mouldy bits of string.

'It's my *ear* that's been hurt!' protested Voxy as they lifted him on to the stretcher. 'I don't *walk* with my ears!'

But Frazzle and Spit began racing across the valley floor, carrying the stretcher, with Robbie right behind them. Up the Zorb mountain they puffed and along several paths, until they reached the hospital in a field full of the spiky red grass. A large square of grass had been flattened and three rows of sunken mud beds dug into the ground. The beds contained Zorbs with a range of injuries, from snout bruising to twisted claws. They were all covered with canopy-leaf sheets.

The hospital was surrounded by the bases of several tree trunks, each of which contained bottles and tubes of various medical lotions and potions, like *Extra-Frothy Ear Wax Extractor* and *Ultra-Fine Tail Cleanser*.

Voxy groaned when he saw Matron Bab. She was trying to pull a boulder out of an older Zorb warrior's nose, with some kind of giant blue chopsticks. When she heard Voxy and co. turn up, she handed the chopsticks over to the Zorb and bustled over to greet her new arrivals.

'Tip him on to Bed 14!' she commanded. Frazzle and Spit lowered Voxy into one of the mud beds and then headed back towards the valley.

Matron Bab lifted Voxy's injured ear.

'A perforation in Ear Section 3!' she declared 'You'll need twenty-four hours of bed rest before we can stitch you up.'

'Twenty-four hours!' groaned Voxy. 'But ... that means I'll miss all of tomorrow's battle!'

'Tough luck!' replied Matron, hurrying back to her boulder-up-nostril patient.

Robbie and a very forlorn Voxy sat in silence for a few minutes.

'I still don't get it,' said Robbie eventually. 'When humans fight wars there's usually a reason. It's always over land or water or their leaders calling each other names – things like that.'

'I've told you,' sighed Voxy. 'The boulders fall from the trees. We collect the boulders. We store them up. And then we fight.'

'What did you just say?' asked Robbie, his ears suddenly pricking up.

'... And then we fight,' replied Voxy.

'No, the bit about them falling off trees.'

'That's where we get them. Those bare knobbly trees in the valley. They bloom in spring. That's when we collect the boulders.'

Robbie slapped the palm of his right hand against his forehead. 'Why didn't you tell me that earlier?' he demanded.

'You didn't ask,' said Voxy.

Robbie was about to speak again but he felt a painful whack on the shoulder.

'Visiting time is over!' barked Matron Bab, pulling back her tail to hit him again.

'Just a few more minutes,' pleaded Robbie.

But Matron lifted Robbie up with her ears and hurled him through the air. He landed with a bump about twenty feet away in the tall, spiky grass.

'You may see him when visiting time starts at 11 a.m. tomorrow!' she called after him. 'But until then, you STAY AWAY!'

Robbie stood up, brushed himself down and hurried off, buzzing with the plan that was forming in his brain.

'P^{ssst, Voxy!'}

It was much later. The sky was a dark bluey-black and a silence had fallen over the valley. Day One of the Boulder Battle was over. It had ended with both sides being 63 warriors down, with 37 still standing. Taking into account those injured warriors who weren't too seriously hurt, each side would be able to field about 60 warriors for Boulder Battle Day Two.

The only light in the field hospital was a pale glow coming from a light in one of the tree trunks. Matron Bab was nowhere to be seen.

'*Voxy, wake up!*'

Voxy let out a snore, and mumbled, 'Feed me some sour cabbage and soil burgers.'

In desperation, Robbie tugged the fur on his friend's undamaged ear.

Voxy's eyes opened. 'Is it breakfast yet?' he asked.

'Get out of bed now!' ordered Robbie.

'What's going on?' yawned Voxy, sleepily climbing out of bed. The fur around his damaged ear hole was pulsing brightly.

'We're on a mission,' whispered Robbie.

Satisfied that Matron wasn't around, Robbie led a yawning Voxy past the other beds and out into the night.

'Where are we going?' asked Voxy, as they ran through another of the bubbly green swamps. Robbie said nothing until he pulled up next to Voxy's school.

'Isn't it a bit late for a game of Melafon?' asked Voxy, rubbing his eyes.

But Robbie went past the school and stopped outside the Junk Store.

'Er, this place is totally out of bounds,' said Voxy. 'I told you, if we try to go in and anyone sees us, we're dead!'

'No one will know,' said Robbie. 'Now help me up.'

Voxy leaned down and Robbie climbed on to his back.

'What do you want in *there*?' asked Voxy.

'I'll tell you in a minute,' replied Robbie, easing himself on to the roof. It was covered in large, old rusty tiles that creaked under his weight.

'I won't be long,' he called to Voxy. 'Wait there and whatever you do, DON'T follow me!'

Voxy frowned, desperate to know what Robbie was up to.

Robbie crawled across the roof until he found a loose tile. Very carefully, he slid it aside and lowered himself into the hole, clinging to the other roof tiles with his hands. It was incredibly dark inside the Junk Store, so Robbie was pleased he'd brought his torch along. He shone it down and saw an old sofa made from twigs and bales of the red spiky grass. He took a deep breath and let go of the roof tiles.

His fall was broken by the twig and grass sofa. He climbed off it and moved his torch in large sweeping arcs. The Junk Store was the right name for the place – wherever you looked there was ... junk. Robbie saw huge pieces of smashed metal machinery, broken pipes made from bark, great mounds of reddish earth and a pile of smashed-up traditional Zorb battle shields.

He spent the next ten minutes turning things over and putting them back – some half-finished Zorb bikes with seven and a half wheels, a stack of ear-grooming kits that were ten years out of date, and several dozen broken packs of elastic-eyebrow cutters. He was just starting to get

frustrated when he finally found what he was looking for – a long line of dust-covered books.

He flicked through them and put the first twenty to one side. But he struck gold with the twenty-first. He opened the book and scanned the contents page. He flipped to page 124 and read the first three paragraphs.

Jackpot!

He was about to go on reading when a huge crash sounded behind him, making him jump in fright.

Through a big dust cloud came Voxy.

'I told you not to follow me!' hissed Robbie.

'I got bored of waiting,' replied Voxy. 'WHAT'S GOING ON?'

Robbie was about to explain when another sound erupted. But this one was a voice; the voice of Captain Prush.

'WHAT ON EARTH ARE YOU TWO DOING IN HERE?' he demanded furiously.

'We could ask you the same question,' said Voxy quickly, pointing to the pile of letters the Captain was holding tightly in his claws.

Prush's cheeks turned purple. 'Erm ... these ... are ... er ... you go first!'

'OK,' said Robbie, eyeing Prush. 'I think it's crazy that young Zorbs don't learn to read. I came in here to see if there were any books that could help me teach Voxy.'

The Captain pursed his lips.

'Your turn,' said Voxy.

Prush coughed. 'Well, er ... the thing is,' he began, trying hard not to blush any more, 'since we ... have been in touch with the human world, I have very much enjoyed listening to the music of Anvilla Egghead and the Gazelles of Death. I heard them on human radio.'

Robbie stared at the Captain in amazement.

'I've become a massive fan of Anvilla,' went on the Captain, 'and I started writing letters to her several weeks ago asking for her ... autograph. But all of my letters have been sent back with no reply. That has been very, very disappointing. Why won't she reply, even to just one of my letters?'

'And you're keeping all of the returned letters in here?' asked Robbie.

Prush nodded. 'I don't want anyone else to

see them. I feel foolish about the whole thing.'

There was silence inside the dim light of the Junk Store for a few seconds.

'Can I see one of them?' asked Robbie.

Prush shrugged his shoulders and handed one over.

Robbie shone his torch at the address on the front of the envelope.

Anvila Eghed
The Hooman Setlement
Earf

Robbie had to stop himself from laughing.

'Are you mocking me?' demanded the Captain, seeing the twinkle in Robbie's eyes.

'Of course not,' replied Robbie, 'it's just that humans don't all live in *one* settlement. There are billions of us, so we live in loads of different places. Our addresses have numbers, street names, postcodes and countries. That's why they've all been sent back. With the address you've been using, your letters never reached her.'

'Oh,' said Captain Prush, looking very embarrassed. 'I thought her not replying meant that humans are nasty creatures – creatures you can't trust.'

'So that's why you've been ultra-mean to Robbie ever since he arrived!' cried Voxy.

Captain Prushkin hung his head in shame.

'I'll tell you what,' said Robbie. 'If you stop being horrible to me, I'll get Anvilla's real address when I get home and send it to you. Then, when you write asking for an autograph, your letter *will* get to her.'

'Would you do that?' asked the Captain excitedly.

Robbie nodded.

'It's a deal,' said Prush, 'but it doesn't mean I'll give you any special treatment on the battlefield tomorrow.'

'I wouldn't expect anything different,' smiled Robbie.

'Good,' nodded Prush. 'I suggest we don't mention this little meeting to anyone.'

Robbie and Voxy nodded.

Prush gazed up at the missing roof panel, looked at Voxy and then held up a key. ' Maybe you should use the door on your way out.'

A mist filled the valley in the early hours of the following morning, but by the time the sun rose, it had cleared for Day Two of the Boulder Battle.

Robbie hurried across the red spiky grass. The rucksack on his back contained the book he'd found in the Junk Store last night. He stopped when he caught sight of the field hospital. Last night it had been pitch black and Matron Bab hadn't been around. Now, bright sunlight streamed through it and there was Matron, marching between the beds and keeping a beady eye on all of her patients.

When she wasn't looking in Voxy's direction, Robbie crouched down and scurried over to his bed.

'Voxy, come on!' he hissed.

'I've been waiting for you,' said Voxy, easing his body over the side of the bed, while Robbie kept an eye on Matron.

But Voxy's tail got caught up in his canopy-leaf sheet. A second later it had wrapped itself around his whole body and he went clattering on to the floor.

Matron Bab spun round. 'WHAT DO YOU THINK YOU'RE DOING?' she bellowed at the sheet-wrapped monster.

'MKLHGGA!' came the muffled sound from inside the sheet.

She then spotted Robbie.

'WHAT ARE *YOU* DOING HERE?' she fumed. 'YOU KNOW VISITING TIME HASN'T STARTED YET!'

'I just—'

But before Robbie could get any more words out of his mouth, Matron Bab began marching towards them. Voxy wriggled round on the floor trying to escape from his sheet, while Robbie desperately looked around for a way of stopping Matron's advance. He spied a large bottle of *Extra-Frothy Ear Wax Extractor* beside the bed next to Voxy's. He quickly grabbed it and as Matron Bab bore down on them, he unscrewed the cap and threw some of the liquid in her path.

The second her feet came into contact with the frothy pool, they skidded forward and she flew up into the air. She came down on her backside with a mighty bump and was sent shooting backwards across the hospital floor.

'COME ON, VOXY – LET'S GO!' shouted Robbie.

'KOGFDV!!' came the reply from inside the sheet.

Robbie snatched at the sheet and tried to untwist it, but it didn't work. Matron was whizzing faster and faster across the floor.

Robbie suddenly had a brainwave. 'BITE IT!' he shouted.

Voxy obviously got the message, as a few seconds later he started ripping the sheet to shreds with his teeth. Robbie pulled at the shreds and finally Voxy was free. He and Robbie jumped to their feet and ran.

'STOP RIGHT THERE!' shrieked Matron

as she crashed into the base of a tree trunk medicine chest.

But they sprinted on and didn't look back.

'WE NEED TO SPEED UP!' shouted Robbie as their feet pounded through the red spiky grass. As they approached the mud bowl they heard two things – the squawking call of the bird followed by Captain Prush yelling, 'CHARGE!'

'WE'RE TOO LATE!' groaned Voxy.

'WE CAN STILL DO IT!' shouted Robbie.

They flew across the mud bowl to the tip of the Zorb mountain and saw the two sets of warriors thundering down into the valley.

'We'll never catch them!' panted Voxy, 'and as soon as the battle starts, we won't have a chance!'

But Robbie had an idea. 'How far does your tail go at full stretch?'

'You don't mean ...' asked Voxy.

'How far?' repeated Robbie.

'I don't know,' said Voxy, 'I've never tried it.'

'Well, now's the time to find out!'

The two monster armies were now halfway down their mountains, and it would be a matter of seconds before the day's battle began.

'It's too dangerous!' said Voxy.

'There's no other way!' replied Robbie, running across to a jutting-out section of the mountaintop with a sheer drop below.

Voxy took a very deep breath, ran over to Robbie and started unwinding his tail. Robbie grabbed it with both hands.

'This is crazy!' shouted Voxy.

But Robbie ran backwards and with a giant shout of 'HERE GOES!' threw himself over the edge of the mountain. The wind whipped past his ears as he crashed downwards.

Forget fairground rides! This is the way to travel!

But when he looked down, his spirits sank. The two armies had almost reached the valley

floor and Voxy's tail was a long way from the
bottom.

He looked up and saw Voxy's anxious face
peering down over the mountaintop.

'FASTER!' yelled Robbie.

With a great whooshing sound, Voxy's tail suddenly went at twice the speed. It was so fast that Robbie almost lost his grip, but somehow he managed to hold on.

The troops had now reached the valley floor and were racing towards each other, screaming and shouting, boulders at the ready.

With the ground only fifteen feet away, Robbie slammed the soles of his feet against the side of the mountain and pushed off, at the same time as letting go of Voxy's tail with his hands.

He bent his knees and landed with a crash, right between the two fast-approaching armies, letting out the loudest yell he had ever yelled. And the single word he yelled was:

10

To Robbie's amazement, instead of mowing him down, both armies skidded to a thundering halt, just five feet apart, with him standing directly in between them.

'GET OUT OF THE WAY!' yelled Captain Prush. 'WE HAVE A BATTLE TO FIGHT!'

'HEAR, HEAR!' shrieked Captain Mulch. 'CLEAR THE ROUTE!'

'SOMEONE GIVE ME A BOULDER!' shouted Robbie.

'WHY?' demanded Prush, whose face had turned purple with rage.

'JUST GIVE ME ONE!' insisted Robbie.

There was a lot of murmuring, until a Zorb warrior threw him a boulder. Robbie caught it. From his rucksack he pulled out a makeshift knife he'd made from the metal off-cuts of his new shields. He held the knife in the air and plunged it into the boulder.

There was a sharp intake of breath from both sides.

With some effort Robbie sliced through the boulder's leathery skin and cut it in half. He held up the two halves to show both armies the red, gooey stuff inside. He scooped some out and dropped it into his mouth.

'WHAT THE ...?' chorused the astonished warriors.

Robbie quickly pulled out the book he'd found in the Junk Store. 'YOU WANT TO KNOW WHY YOU FIGHT THIS BATTLE?' he cried.

Prush and Mulch snorted at him angrily, but

lots of warriors on both sides nodded. Robbie
held up the book and began to read:

*In ancient times three tiny Ferfel
trees grew in the valley between
the Zorb and Grobble settlements.*

These trees produced the delicious red Ferfel fruit, or 'Boulders' as they were called – because they looked like boulders.

'FRUIT!' exclaimed the monsters in surprise.

'IT REALLY IS DELICIOUS!' shouted Robbie, wiping some juice off his lips, before continuing.

As the trees were right in the middle of the valley, the Zorbs and the Grobbles argued over who owned the trees. Because they couldn't agree, they started throwing the Ferfel 'Boulders' at each other.

The monsters' mouths hung open in amazement.

Realizing they couldn't fight every day, the Zorbs and the Grobbles decided *to stage a two-day Boulder Battle each year. At the end of the battle, the clan with the most warriors standing would get to eat all of the valley's Ferfel fruit, and be in charge of the valley floor, for a whole year – until the fruit had grown back and it was time for the next battle. This became a tradition.*

'THERE YOU GO!' shouted Captain Prush. 'IT'S A TRADITION. TRADITIONS NEED TO BE CONTINUED!'

'NO!' shouted Robbie. 'LOOK AROUND YOU!'

Prush, Mulch and all of the other warriors looked around the valley floor at the large number of knobbly trees.

'CAN'T YOU SEE!' cried Robbie. 'BACK THEN THERE WERE ONLY *THREE* FERFEL FRUIT TREES. NOW THERE ARE WELL OVER A HUNDRED!'

At that second, Voxy came crashing down into the valley. 'How's it going?' he shouted.

'I've just got to the part where I tell them that the original reason for fighting the battle doesn't apply any more,' called out Robbie.

'WELL, WHAT ARE YOU WAITING FOR?' cried Voxy at both armies. 'THERE'S PLENTY OF FRUIT FOR EVERYONE! THE BATTLE IS OVER! LET THE FEAST BEGIN!'

There was a hushed silence in the valley that seemed to go on forever.

And then Captain Prush finally spoke. 'A good soldier *never* fights a pointless war,' he said quietly. He swallowed deeply and then took a few hesitant steps towards Captain Mulch. The two battle-hardened warriors eyed each other up and down. Then, as if in slow motion, they hesitantly shook claws.

There was a huge gasp of astonishment from both armies and then another long silence.

But then slowly, very slowly, the Zorbs and

Grobbles started moving towards each other. They began with shy claw-to-fist shakes, but after a few minutes of this some of them began patting each other on the shoulders. This gradually led to tapping each other's bellies and finally, giving each other great big monster hugs.

It wasn't long before the valley rang out with cheers and laughter. Robbie and Voxy raced round, cutting open boulder after boulder with Robbie's makeshift knife. Soon the sound of slurping, chewing and gargling could be heard as everyone tried the deliciously juicy red Ferfel fruit. The celebrations stopped for a moment when Matron Bab thundered into the valley yelling she'd get revenge on Robbie and Voxy. But when Captain Prush explained what had happened, she stuffed several clawfuls of Ferfel fruit into her mouth and began dancing an old Zorb jig.

All of the non-warriors up in the settlements

heard the commotion and came down to find out what all the fuss was about. They were told the incredible story and offered some succulent Ferfel fruit. Before long lots of extra food and drink was brought down into the valley to continue the celebrations.

Voxy's parents ran straight over to Robbie and Voxy.

'We are SO proud of you two!' beamed Voxy's mum, squeezing them both on the shoulders.

'I LOVED my day as a warrior,' sighed Voxy, 'but I know that stopping the fighting was the right thing to do.'

'You're heroes!' cried Voxy's dad, giving his son and Robbie huge slaps on the back. 'Together, you've put an end to the Boulder Battle, and you will always be remembered for that! Thank goodness we agreed to host a human visitor!'

Frazzle and Spit walked past, talking excitedly to each other.

'I love the idea of setting up a Ferfel Fruit Juice Bar in the valley, dude!' said Frazzle.

'Totally!' agreed Spit. 'We can have, like, a menu, and everything!'

A few minutes later, Robbie felt a claw on his shoulder.

He turned round and came face-to-face with Captain Prush.

'I've come to apologize,' said the Captain humbly. 'Not only have you just ended a pointless battle, but Spit tells me it was you who got the Flinger working and you who stopped ten boulders from crashing into my head.'

'No problem,' smiled Robbie, 'and just remember – I'll get you Anvilla Egghead's address.'

'Thank you, dear human boy, thank you!' beamed Prush.

He walked away muttering about how 'kind' and 'trustworthy' humans were.

Voxy looked at Robbie. 'You know that thing you said to Prush in the Junk Store, about teaching me to read, did you mean it?

'Nah,' replied Robbie, 'unless you really want to learn.'

Voxy thought this over. 'Maybe,' he said, 'but first there's something you HAVE to try back at my place.'

*

As yet another toast was drunk to the glorious taste of the Ferfel fruit and the end of the Boulder Battle, Robbie and Voxy quietly slipped away.

'What do I HAVE to try?' asked Robbie.

'It's my dad's porcupine stew,' grinned Voxy, 'the tastiest snack in the world!'

During his stay with the Zorbs, Robbie had made a huge effort to eat all of the strange food that had been placed before him. At that moment though, his idea of a tasty snack and Voxy's idea of one weren't quite the same.

It had been an incredible visit – one that

Robbie Percival would NEVER forget. But as he and his monster friend ran up the Zorb mountain, one enormous question floated through the air, like the droppings of a Pelgo bird (only far less smelly).

What on EARTH would happen when Voxy visited Robbie's world?

VOXY
and the
CRAZY
CAMPING
TRIP

Dear Robbie and family

I am delighted you have agreed to host the visit of Voxy – a monster from the Zorb monster clan.

At the start, I should point out that Zorb habits are quite different from human ones. For example, Zorbs do **NOT** like sleeping on flat surfaces. They prefer sleeping in mud beds sunk into the ground. If you 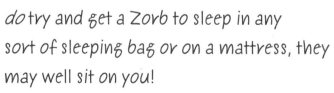 do try and get a Zorb to sleep in any sort of sleeping bag or on a mattress, they may well sit on you!

Also, in the Zorb world, if you get mud ketchup on your face, you don't wipe it

away with a napkin; one of your fellow
monsters licks it off.
I do not expect you
to lick ketchup off
Voxy's face, but
please don't be too
surprised if
he licks it off
yours.

I hope Voxy's visit goes extremely well.
    With very best wishes

Sir Horace Upton

Human Agency for Understanding Monsters

1

One second the harbour was quiet, the sun glinting over its gentle, lapping water; the next, a large white boat crashed into view, being tugged by a huge light blue monster, swimming on its front at crazy speed. The boat zigzagged between a line of tall red yachts and then kicked up a huge wave as it juddered to a halt by the jetty.

The ship's captain, whose white hair was matched by his very pale face, jumped off the boat and ran away as fast as he could.

'BUT YOU WERE GOING WAY TOO

SLOW!' shouted the monster after him.

'VOXY!' cried Robbie Percival, running towards the monster, who was busy shaking water off his fur.

'ROBBIE!' beamed Voxy, giving his human friend a whack on the shoulder with his expanding tail.

Whoever would have thought that a human and a monster – particularly one as huge as Voxy – would have ended up mates? But that's exactly what they were. Robbie had enjoyed an amazing stay in Voxy's monster settlement; now it was Voxy's turn to visit Robbie.

Robbie's mum, dad and younger sister, Kat, stared up in amazement at the ten-foot monster with his dark blue, twinkling eyes. They gazed at his bushy eyebrows with their curly strands; they gaped at his two seven-fingered claws and puffed-up webbed feet.

'Hello, Voxy, I'm George Percival,' said Robbie's dad, stepping forward.

'And I'm Linda – Robbie's mum,' smiled Mrs Percival, giving Voxy a small wave.

'Mr and Mrs P!' shouted Voxy. Shooting out his wafer-thin ears, he grabbed them – one with each ear – and spun them round in circles.

'Woooooaaaahhh!' cried Mr and Mrs Percival.

When Voxy finally let go, they carried on twirling for several minutes.

'What a ... lovely greeting,' said Robbie's mum dizzily, when she finally stopped spinning.

'I'm Kat,' said Robbie's sister, stepping back because she didn't want to be whacked by Voxy's tale or spun round by his giant ears.

'Hey, Kat! Greetings, Percival family!' cried Voxy. 'Now come on, Robbie, tell me all about this outdoor thingy we're going on!'

'It's called the Rackham Forest Camp-Out Challenge,' said Robbie, leading Voxy to the Percivals' car.

'A *Challenge*?' said Voxy. 'Do we get to bash anyone?'

'Er ... not exactly,' replied Robbie's dad.

Voxy looked disappointed.

'But we do get to compete against loads of other families, in all these outdoor events,' explained Kat. 'Like climbing trees on home-made rope ladders and canoeing with pine-cone oars!'

'Last year we came third,' said Robbie.

'THIRD!' exclaimed Voxy. 'Third is RUBBISH! This year Team Percival has to *win*!'

'Yeah!' laughed Robbie, doing a hand-to-claw high five with Voxy.

'We bought the biggest trailer we could find,' said Robbie's dad when they reached the car.

Voxy jumped up on to the giant steel trailer fixed to the back of the Percivals' car, and started stomping up and down, making several large dents in its surface.

'Er ... I think it's probably better if you sit down,' said Robbie's dad nervously.

'No worries, Mr P!' nodded Voxy, leaping into the air and falling down with a crash. Robbie climbed in next to him and did up both of their seatbelts. Mr and Mrs Percival and Kat got into the car.

A few seconds later they were off.

'This is EXCELLENT!' laughed Voxy as the car sped up the motorway. Lots of other cars hooted, their passengers pointing and gasping at the Percivals' remarkable passenger. One man was so fascinated by Voxy that his wife had to hit him over the head with a road atlas, to remind him to drive forwards not sideways.

'Here are some snacks that Robbie made!' called Kat, passing out a bag of crisps.

'One of my best flavours!' shouted Robbie. 'Sultana and Dandelion!' Robbie fancied himself as the world's number one crisp inventor.

Voxy frowned at the smallness of the bag.

'Don't worry,' said Robbie, 'these ones are for me. Yours are coming!'

Kat passed out a pack that was ten times bigger.

Voxy grabbed it and tipped the whole thing, packet and all, straight into his mouth. He chewed for a minute or two. 'The crisps taste OK,' he said, munching very loudly and showering crisp crumbs everywhere, 'but the *packet* was delicious. 'Have you got any more?'

But before Robbie could answer, the car suddenly started slowing down.

'Are we there?' asked Voxy excitedly.

Robbie looked over the side of the trailer. 'It's a traffic jam!' he groaned. 'We'll be late for the first event!'

'Not if I can help it!' shouted Voxy, unclipping his seatbelt and jumping on to the tarmac. He ran to the front of the Percivals' car and in one swift move lifted it and the trailer on to his back. A second later he was running down the hard shoulder of the motorway.

'AAAAAAAAAAAHHHHHH!' screamed Robbie's parents and Kat, grabbing hold of anything they could inside the car.

'AWESOME!' shouted Robbie, bouncing up and down in the trailer.

Voxy sped on, passing hundreds of cars and thousands of astonished onlookers. He looked round and saw Robbie's parents and Kat flapping about in the car with very green faces.

That must be the colour humans go when they're having amazing fun, thought Voxy.

But then he spotted a blue and white car racing up the hard shoulder behind him, a red light flashing on its roof.

'THIS IS THE POLICE!' boomed a megaphone voice from inside the car.

'WE ORDER YOU TO STOP IMMEDIATELY!!!'

Voxy screeched to a halt and lowered the Percivals' car and trailer down on to the road.

'Who are these warriors?' asked Voxy. 'Shall I attack them?'

'NO!' cried the Percivals.

One of the policemen put on his helmet and got out of the car. He walked over to the Percivals' car and stared up at Voxy with his mouth open.

'Something wrong, officer?' asked Mr Percival, winding down his window.

'It seems that a very large monster has been carrying your car and trailer down the hard shoulder of the motorway,' said the policeman.

'He's called Voxy and he's on an official visit,' said Robbie, jumping out of the trailer. 'It's organized by the Human Agency for Understanding Monsters!' He waved Sir Horace Upton's letter in the policeman's face.

'That's right!' nodded Voxy, 'I'm *official.*'

The policeman's body jolted in shock. 'He … he … can speak?'

'Of course I can speak,' said Voxy.

The policeman gulped.

'We're actually on our way to the Rackham Forest Camp-Out Challenge,' explained Mrs Percival.

'And we're going to be late,' tutted Voxy.

'Think how bad that will look to the monster world!' cried Robbie. 'They'll think humans can't organize anything.'

'You're right!' nodded the policeman. 'It will look terrible!'

He paused for a moment, then spun round and ran back to the police car. 'They've got an official monster in their trailer!' he shouted. 'We need to get them all to Rackham Forest as quick as possible!'

'No problem!' cried the other officer, firing up the police car's engine.

And so, instead of crawling through miles of traffic, or being carried by a ten-foot Zorb monster, the Percivals (and Voxy) were escorted down the hard shoulder, past thousands of stationary vehicles, by a gleaming police car with flashing lights and a wailing siren.

Half an hour later, they reached Rackham Forest.

'GOOD LUCK!' beamed the first policeman, holding open the gate to the camping field.

'You're bound to do well with Mr Voxy on

122

your side!' saluted the second officer.

Voxy beamed with pride and waved his paw as if he was a monster king.

The Percivals' car bumped over the field. All around people were spreading out ground sheets, hammering in tent pegs and tying up guy ropes. Most people were too busy setting up their tents to notice the new arrivals, but as everyone had been told there would be a special contestant on one of the teams, those who did see Voxy gave him a welcoming wave.

Mr Percival parked the car next to a hedge by a large open space, that was flanked on either side by big tents belonging to other families.

'Right,' said Mrs Percival, 'Robbie and Voxy, you put up your tent. Me, Dad and Kat will put up ours.'

'I designed this tent especially for you,' said Robbie, grabbing two big bags from the trailer and pulling out some giant bendy poles, loads of tent pegs and several large sheets of orange canvas. 'There's a big hole in the floor for you to dig a mud bed!'

'Nice one!' grinned Voxy.

They slotted the bendy poles through holes in the canvas. Voxy then held up the poles while Robbie secured them with tent pegs. Next Voxy used his eyebrows to clip on the main part of the tent and the flysheet. Finally he hammered in the outer pegs with his tail, while Robbie fastened the guy ropes.

'Let's check it out!' shouted Voxy, diving inside. He dug a deep and comfortable mud bed for himself in the floor hole. 'Do you want me to dig one for you?' he asked.

'No thanks,' replied Robbie, stepping inside. 'I'll be fine with my sleeping bag.'

They hung out for a few minutes until the noise of angry voices drew them outside.

The other tent was still lying in pieces on the ground.

'No!' Robbie's mum was saying. 'That big blue pole goes there!'

'I think you're reading those instructions upside down,' replied Robbie's dad.

'You're both wrong!' said Kat.

'Shall we ...?' whispered Voxy.

Robbie nodded.

Silently, they grabbed all of the gear and with the help of Voxy's ears, eyebrows and

powerful tail, put up the second tent in less than five minutes, while the rest of Team Percival carried on arguing.

'THERE YOU GO!' declared Robbie.

His parents and Kat looked up from their argument and gazed in astonishment at the completed tent.

'Oh,' said Robbie's dad.

'Ah,' said Robbie's mum.

'Brilliant!' beamed Kat.

The Percivals' tents stood among lots of other tents of every colour, shape and size. A mini canvas city had sprouted up in a field that had been empty a few hours ago.

'If we want to toast marshmallows on a fire tonight, we'll need to get some wood,' said Robbie's mum.

'I like the sound of toasted marshmallows!' cried Voxy. 'How many can you eat at once?'

'We normally eat one,' replied Kat, 'but you can have as many as you like.'

Just the kind of answer I like! thought Voxy.

The five of them followed a path that led from the back of their tents into the forest itself. The trees were at least fifty feet tall and rays of sunlight cut between them and shone on to the forest floor.

'First we need little twigs for kindling,' said Robbie's dad, when they came to a clearing, 'then large branches to get the fire going. Let's think BIG!'

Before long they had collected a very large pile of twigs and branches.

'Some of the logs are too big to carry,' said Robbie's mum.

'No they're not!' said Voxy, throwing the biggest log in the air with his snout. As it fell back down, he chopped it into three smaller chunks with his tail.

'Wow!' said Robbie's mum, as Voxy did this with the rest of the big logs.

'There's too much to carry in one go,' said Robbie's dad.

'No there's not!' said Voxy, shooting out some strands from his eyebrows, wrapping them round the entire pile and lifting it up.

'Remarkable!' said Robbie's dad.

The walk back to the camping field was a happy one – everyone looking forward to eating supper, getting stuck into the first event, then roasting marshmallows by a roaring fire. But when they reached the campsite, they stopped dead in their tracks.

Where there had been loads of other tents all around their ones, now there were *none*. Every other tent now stood at the far end of the field.

The Percivals' tents were completely alone.

3

'What on earth is going on?' asked Mr Percival.

'Look!' said Robbie, pointing to a cardboard sign that had been hammered into the ground.

HEALTH + SAFETY NOTICE
FOR THE PERCIVAL FAMILY

It has come to my attention that a dirty great beast will be camping with you in this spot. While some of the other contestants seemed to think this was OK, I have explained to them that the creature is probably diseased and full of germs and poses a risk to their health and the health of their children. I have therefore advised everyone to move their tents as far away from yours as possible.

PERCIVALS - YOU HAVE BEEN WARNED!

Mr T. C. CARLTON

Diseased! thought Voxy crossly. *The worst illness I've ever had was Blue-chicken-toe fungus.*

'Carlton!' cried Robbie. 'That's the name of the most annoying boy in my class!'

'Yeah,' replied Kat, 'and he's heading this way right now!'

'NOOOOOOOOOO!' groaned Robbie, spotting his worst enemy walking towards him.

Ian Carlton was a tall, bony boy with greasy hair and a sneering smile. Striding along beside him were his father and Mr Mills, the Camp-Out Challenge Organizer. Mr Carlton had bright red cheeks and a thick, bushy moustache. Mr Mills was wearing yellow, all-weather clothing, a yellow rain hat and large round glasses perched on the edge of his nose.

'Ian must have overheard me talking about the Camp-Out Challenge at school and got his dad to enter,' said Robbie.

'Ian Carlton is the biggest cheater, worst fouler and most terrible loser in the whole universe,' Kat explained to Voxy.

'The Percivals must get rid of that dirty beast at once!' Mr Carlton was shouting at Mr Mills. 'I bet the rules don't say monsters are allowed to take part in this challenge.'

'Hey!' shouted Robbie, as Ian and the two men reached the Percivals. 'Voxy is part of our family. If he goes, we go!'

'Hear, hear!' shouted the rest of the Percivals.

Mr Mills sighed and pulled some papers labelled **CAMP-OUT CHALLENGE RULES** from his mac pocket. He began flicking through them.

'You're right, Mr Carlton,' he nodded after a couple of minutes. 'The rules don't say that monsters can take part.'

'So boot him out!' shouted Mr Carlton.

'However …' Mr Mills went on, 'they don't say that monsters CAN'T take part. So I rule that Voxy... can stay.'

'YES!' cried Robbie and Voxy, doing a victory dance.

Mr Carlton's cheeks went even redder.

Ian's face crumpled like a punched-in paper bag.

'You haven't heard the last of this!' snapped Mr Carlton, turning on his heels and storming off, with Ian at his side.

You haven't heard the last of this, said Robbie, mimicking Mr Carlton.

You haven't heard the last of this, said Voxy, mimicking Robbie mimicking Mr Carlton.

Mr Mills handed Mrs Percival a list of all the families taking part in the Camp-Out Challenge. Voxy and Robbie looked at it over her shoulder. It listed the Dentons, Jobsons, Watkins, Kahns, Sunderlands, Alis, Percivals and Carltons.

Mr Mills then looked down and saw Mr Carlton's sign on the ground. He frowned, pulled it up and stuffed it into his mac pocket. 'I better be off,' he said. 'The first challenge starts in forty-five minutes.'

'I can't believe Ian and his dad are here!' groaned Robbie.

'Let's forget about the Carltons for a minute and get on with supper,' said Mrs Percival.

'We're having beans on toast,' said Mr Percival. 'Robbie and Voxy – you get the gas grill going and do the toast. Kat, Mum and I will get the plates and cutlery and heat up the beans on the gas stove, OK?'

The gas grill was pretty powerful and Voxy enjoyed turning the pieces of bread with his ears until they were well toasted on both sides. Soon the beans were piping hot and it was time to tuck in.

The four Percivals each got two thick slices of buttered toast and a big helping of beans on their blue camping plates. Voxy had a large white tray, on to which they heaped ten slices of toast and the contents of six cans of beans.

Voxy liked the beans and toast very much but he wolfed the whole lot down in a few mouthfuls.

These humans don't eat very much! he thought.

'Is that it?' he asked, licking some tomato sauce off his snout. He was about to lick some off Kat's face, but Robbie shook his head and Voxy got the message.

'Er, yes,' said Robbie's mum, 'but we do have a large packet of pasta.'

She reached for it and started to open it. 'All we need to do is boil some water and—'

Before she could finish her sentence, Voxy had grabbed the packet and tipped the entire contents into his mouth. His teeth started chomping on the dry pasta tubes.

'Not bad,' he nodded, 'but they could do with some mud ketchup.'

'I'm afraid we don't have any of that,' said Mr Percival.

'No problem,' said Voxy, scooping some mud off the ground and tipping it into his mouth.

After he'd finished the pasta, he ate two whole melons (with their rinds on), seven apples

(including their cores) and the entire weekend's supply of chocolate.

Kat was upset about the chocolate, but her mum promised they'd buy some more tomorrow. A few moments later, Mr Mills' voice rang out through a megaphone.

'Everyone to the log circle!' he called. 'The first event is about to begin!'

'I've just got to nip to the toilet,' said Robbie. 'Voxy, come with me. We'll see you guys in a minute.'

So, as Robbie's parents and Kat strode to the circle, Robbie and Voxy ran over to the washroom block.

'I'll be one minute,' said Robbie, going inside.

Voxy stood in the warm evening air, using his snout to remove a pasta tube that had got stuck between his teeth. Suddenly, he felt a thud on his back. He turned round and saw Ian Carlton sneering up at him.

'Mr Mills may think it's OK for you to take

part in the Camp-Out Challenge,' hissed Ian, 'but me and my dad think it's a disgrace. And anyway, there's no point in you being here. The Percivals haven't got a chance because we're going to win!'

Voxy leaned his head down until it was right in front of Ian's face. 'We'll see about that,' he replied, jiggling his eyebrows.

Ian scowled and started walking away just as Robbie emerged from the washroom.

'What was all that about?' he asked.

'It was nothing,' replied Voxy.

But as they hurried over to the log circle, Voxy got a very uneasy feeling.

Ian and his father mean trouble; BIG trouble.

4

The log circle was in a field next to the campsite. The Percival parents and Kat were sitting on their own, with everyone else bunched up away from them. Mr Carlton had warned them of the risks of sitting anywhere near the 'diseased beast'.

By the time Voxy and Robbie got there, Mr Mills had just finishing telling everyone about the first event.

'What is it?' whispered Robbie.

'We have to make a clay oven and bake our own bread!' replied Kat.

'YES!' mouthed Voxy and Robbie, clenching their claws and fists.

'All of the equipment for this event is set out at the far end of this field,' said Mr Mills.

Everyone looked round and saw big plastic bags set out round the edges of the field at different stations. It was getting dark, so there was a large lantern by each one.

'Each station is marked with a team's name. Are there any questions?'

'Yes,' said Mr Carlton. 'Will you tell us who has won this event immediately after it's finished?'

Mr Mills shook his head. 'I never reveal the winners of individual events. A short while after the final event, I will announce which team has won the overall challenge. I think this makes things more exciting.'

Mr Carlton scowled.

'I suggest we get started,' said Mr Mills, 'so off you go!'

These words had the effect of a starting gun at the Olympics. Every team raced to find their spot. At the Percivals' station Kat quickly tipped out the contents of their plastic bag.

'OK,' she said. 'For the oven we've got mud, straw and water. For the bread we have flour, water, rapid-action yeast and salt. They've also given us some twigs for kindling and some matches. Who's going to do what?'

'Me and Voxy will make the oven,' said Robbie. 'You guys do the bread.'

'Think BIG,' shouted Mr Percival. 'Let's make the *largest* and the *tastiest* loaf!'

A few seconds later, the Percivals and Voxy were all hard at work. Voxy mixed the mud, straw and water into a fine clay. Robbie worked this into a dome-shaped oven, and a clay shelf. The other Percivals made the dough, and created a big loaf. Robbie placed the loaf on the shelf and slotted it into the oven. His dad then lit the twigs at the base of the oven.

During the baking time, Voxy was incredibly useful. He fanned the flames with his tail, and blocked one side of the oven when the wind picked up.

When the loaf was ready, Voxy pulled it out of the oven. It was golden and delicious-smelling. Robbie broke off five tiny bits and passed them round.

'It's good!' nodded Mrs Percival, munching on her piece.

'It's *excellent!*' said Kat.

'Look out, Carltons!' chuckled Voxy.

Mr Percival pulled the shelf out of the oven, placed the loaf back on it and set it down on the ground to cool.

A minute later, Mr Mills announced the event was over and told people to come back to the log circle, leaving their loaves by their ovens.

'I'll catch you up,' said Voxy, who was trying to untangle some large chunks of wet flour that had got twisted up in the fur on his chest.

'Do you want me to help you?' asked Robbie.

'Nah,' replied Voxy, 'I'll be fine.'

So Robbie headed off to the log circle with his parents and Kat.

'Right!' announced Mr Mills when everyone had gathered. 'We'll wait a few minutes for the bread to cool down and then I'll visit each oven and taste all of your loaves.'

So after a brief pause, he set off with everyone right behind him.

First he tried the Watkins family's bread.

'A bit yeasty,' he murmured.

The Dentons' loaf was next.

'A bit salty,' he mumbled.

Then came the Kahns' offering.

'A bit floury,' said Mr Mills.

The Jobsons' bread was 'a bit uncooked', the Alis' was 'a bit muddy' and the Sunderlands' was 'a bit earthy'.

Next up was the Carltons' loaf. Mr Mills broke off a piece and popped it into his mouth. A big smile formed on his lips and he took a deep, satisfied sigh. 'Absolutely delicious!' he said.

Ian Carlton and his father beamed at each other.

'You haven't tasted ours yet,' pointed out Robbie.

'And where exactly *is* the Percival loaf?' asked

Mr Mills when he reached their station.

'It's on the shelf cooling down,' said Robbie, pushing his way through the crowd. But when he reached Mr Mills, his mouth dropped open. The cooling shelf was empty.

The Percivals' loaf had vanished.

'The Carltons must have taken it!' yelled Robbie furiously.

'It wasn't them,' said a deep, growly voice, 'it was me.'

Robbie swung round and saw that the voice belonged to ... Voxy.

'You ate it ALL?' cried Robbie.

'After I'd untangled that wet flour from my fur, I was still hungry,' confessed Voxy, 'so I took a bite of the bread. It tasted so good that I ate another piece and then another ...'

Voxy hung his head in shame.

Maybe I should have left a few crumbs.

There was silence for a few moments and then Mr Carlton burst out laughing. 'Did you hear that, everyone?' he screeched. 'The greedy beast snaffled the whole thing!'

No one else laughed. They went back to their stations to clear up.

'Don't worry,' said Robbie's mum, patting Voxy on the arm.

'It's *our* fault,' said Robbie's dad. 'We should have given you more to eat at supper.'

'It was only a loaf of bread,' said Kat.

'Anyway, there are loads more events,' said Robbie (trying to hide his disappointment). 'And besides, the Carltons' loaf looked *too* good. I reckon they cheated!'

'Now, now,' said his dad. 'The Carltons have behaved very badly, but that doesn't mean they're cheats.'

Voxy was upset for the next hour, but by the time the Percivals had built a fire and started roasting marshmallows, he'd cheered up a lot – helped by the fact that he could squeeze sixteen marshmallows into his mouth at one time. By bedtime, he was back to his normal high spirits, and he snuggled down into his mud bed, looking forward to the next day's events.

*

'Quick! Get over here!' hissed Voxy, giving Robbie a nudge in the ribs with his tail.

149

Robbie yawned, got out of his sleeping bag and joined his monster pal at the door of the tent. He checked his watch. 'It's only 6.50 a.m.,' he muttered. 'What's going on?'

Voxy pointed his snout at the other side of the field. Ian Carlton and his father were hurrying towards the main gate, looking guiltily over their shoulders.

'They're up to something,' said Voxy, 'I'm sure of it!'

'You may be right!' said Robbie, suddenly feeling very awake. 'They may be going to meet a secret accomplice who's camping nearby and helping them cheat!'

A minute later, Voxy and Robbie were running across the field and through the gate. The Carltons were up ahead of them, walking quickly down the lane. Voxy and Robbie hung back and every time the Carltons looked round, they threw themselves against the bank at the side of the road. But when they rounded a

corner and saw the Carltons' destination, they were both very disappointed. The Carltons were entering Mrs Earnshaw's store, the only shop in the local village.

'I don't think Mrs Earnshaw is going to be their accomplice,' said Robbie.

They hid behind a tree and a few minutes later the Carltons came out. Mr Carlton was carrying a blue plastic bag. Voxy and Robbie could just about make out a pint of milk, a loaf of bread and some kind of tube inside.

'Looks like a pack of sweets,' said Robbie.

'What's that piece of paper Mr Carlton's holding?' asked Voxy.

'It's just the till receipt,' answered Robbie. 'It will list all of the things they bought.'

Mr Carlton and Ian set off back towards the site.

'OK,' said Voxy, a minute later. 'I suppose we better get going.'

'Wait a minute,' said Robbie. He quickly ran

into the shop and bought some chocolate for Kat.

When they got back to the site they saw Mr Carlton deep in conversation with Mr Mills. But when Ian appeared as if from nowhere, Mr Carlton suddenly lost interest in talking to Mr Mills and hurried off with his son.

A few minutes later, Mr Mills' voice rang out through his megaphone. 'I am about to hand each team a map for our next challenge – which is a treasure hunt!'

'I LOVE treasure hunts!' exclaimed Voxy. 'Do you think the prize will be a year's supply of Dung Drops?'

'Unlikely,' replied Mrs Percival, 'although you never know.'

'When I give you your map you will also get your first clue,' declared Mr Mills. 'This will lead you to your first stop. Here you will find some coloured stars. Take one of these. There will also be a second clue that will lead you to your second stop where a different-coloured set of stars will be. In all, there are ten stops and ten stars to collect.'

There was excited murmuring among the teams.

'I should add,' went on Mr Mills, 'that each team will be been given their clues in a *different* order, so that no team can follow any other team, and cheat!'

Voxy and Robbie glanced at the Carltons.

A couple of minutes later everyone had been given their maps. These were in thick waterproof, see-through plastic folders.

'The treasure hunt begins NOW!' called Mr Mills.

'I think I should map read,' said Mrs Percival.

'Remember the tent instructions?' replied Mr Percival.

'*I'll* read the map,' said Robbie, snatching it from his mum and working out the first clue. 'Our first stop is this way,' he announced, heading towards the forest.

'What's that?' asked Voxy, pointing out a large bluey-white area on the map, surrounded by squiggly lines.

'Looks like a lake,' replied Robbie.

Half an hour later, the Percivals and Voxy were feeling great. They'd solved the first three clues, found their first three stops and collected a blue, green and red star.

'Next it's over that stile,' said Robbie, checking the map. 'Our fourth star should be on a giant oak tree at the bottom of the field.'

The Percivals climbed over the stile; Voxy jumped it.

'The tree should be right ... over there,' instructed Robbie, walking just behind the others, looking down at the map.

'Why are we stopping?' he asked when he bumped into Voxy, Kat and his parents, who had suddenly halted.

He looked up and saw why.

Coming out from a thick clump of bushes at the bottom of the field was a group of eight bulls. They didn't look too happy that Team Percival were in their field.

'It's OK,' said Robbie's mum calmly. 'If we start walking backwards very slowly, the bulls will see we mean no harm and leave us alone.'

Unfortunately, she was wrong.

Because one second later, the bulls snorted, lowered their heads, and charged.

6

The Percivals screamed and turned to flee as the bulls charged up the field. But Voxy shot out four wire-thin strands from his eyebrows. These zipped towards the fence around the edge of the field, curled round its wooden posts like lassos and stayed firm.

'Everyone jump up and grab one of these!' he shouted, kneeling down so that the Percivals could reach the strands.

Robbie's parents and Kat jumped up and grabbed a strand each.

'AND YOU, ROBBIE!' commanded Voxy.

'I'M NOT GOING WITHOUT YOU!' yelled Robbie.

'I'M A BIG MONSTER AND I CAN LOOK AFTER MYSELF!' bellowed Voxy.

Robbie hesitated, but as the bulls crashed nearer, he jumped up and grabbed the fourth strand. Voxy then raised himself to his full height and flung the Percivals skywards. They whizzed through the air right up to and *over* the fence, where they landed very comfortably on a huge bale of hay.

Voxy then turned to the bulls. *So you lot think you can take on a Zorb monster, do you?*

He extended his tail and started spinning it round.

Faster and faster it went until it looked like a helicopter propeller. Suddenly it was the bulls' turn to be scared. They skidded to a halt and jostled each other, back-pedalling, to get away from the tail-propeller.

Voxy took a step towards them.

That did it.

They snorted in terror and charged back down the field. They didn't stop until they were safely behind their clump of bushes.

'VOXY IS OUR HERO! VOXY IS OUR HERO!' chanted Robbie and Kat as Voxy walked up the field to re-join the Percivals.

'Without you, we'd have been flattened to pancakes!' cried Mr Percival, patting Voxy on the shoulder.

Robbie's mum was looking at the map and frowning. 'Mr Mills would never have sent us into a field of bulls,' she said.

'He must have made a mistake when drawing our route,' replied Robbie, grabbing the map back. 'Let's pick up the trail again.'

At that moment the Carltons appeared over the crest of a hill. 'How many stars have you lot got?' shouted Ian smugly.

'Three,' replied Robbie proudly.

'Three!' sneered Mr Carlton. 'We have SIX!'

'Yeah!' said Ian. We're going to smash you!'

Maybe I should eat the Carltons, thought Voxy. *On second thoughts, they'd probably taste disgusting!*

It took Team Percival another hour to collect all ten stars. They were pleased with their efforts but were still confused about being sent into the field of bulls. Mr Percival tried to discuss this with Mr Mills, but he was too busy getting things ready for the next event.

After a lunch of cheese and pickle sandwiches (Voxy ate sixteen), grape and coffee-flavoured crisps (made by Robbie – Voxy had twelve packs) and fruit (Voxy gobbled nine oranges and a stray lemon), Robbie went to fill up a water container. When he came back, Voxy wasn't around.

'Where is he?' asked Robbie.

'He's just having a go with your camera,' replied Kat.

Robbie tensed. His camera – an X16 V11 Spark Flash Camera – was the one thing he *forbade* other people from using. He spied Voxy near the main gate, clutching the camera with his extended tail and swinging it all over the field. It was weaving in between people's tents, over their cars and up trees.

'VOXY!' shouted Robbie, running across the field, terrified his camera might be broken.

Fortunately, the camera was fine.

'I hope you don't mind that I borrowed it,' said Voxy, handing it back, 'I only took a few shots.'

Robbie checked the display and saw that Voxy had actually taken *seven hundred and twenty-two* photos.

'No problem,' replied Robbie. 'Later on, we'll delete the bad ones and keep the good ones, OK?'

'Brilliant!' agreed Voxy. 'But now it's time for me to teach you the famous Zorb game of Melafon. Come on!'

They ran to a large clear space in the middle of the field, Voxy picking up an old tennis ball he found in the grass, on the way.

'OK,' said Voxy, 'here's how Melafon works. One team are the Lobbers. They throw the Mela, which is a big pink ball. This ball,' he said, holding up the tennis ball, 'will do for a Mela today. The other team are the Flickers. Their job is to hit the Mela from the Flicking Spot with their ears, as far away as possible. They then have to run round three posts and get back to the Flicking Spot without getting hit by the Mela on the backside. If they do this, they score a Fon.'

'Baseball's a bit like that,' nodded Robbie, 'but without the ear-hitting and bum-whacking bits.'

Voxy and Robbie took turns to be the Flicker and the Lobber. Voxy used his ears to whack the tennis ball Mela; Robbie used a long piece of wood. Several kids from the other families drifted over to watch, but their parents arrived and led them away, muttering about germs and disease.

Voxy and Robbie played on, getting more and more involved in the game, but when they heard Mr Mills' megaphone voice, they knew it was time to stop.

'EVERYONE UP AT THE RIVER RACK IN WATERPROOFS, IN FIFTEEN MINUTES!' boomed Mr Mills.

'FOR THE HARDEST, MOST DAREDEVIL EVENT YET!'

7

Fifteen minutes later, everyone was standing beside the fast-flowing River Rack. The white foam of the current bubbled and frothed between the banks of short grass, leading the river downstream, before rounding a bend and snaking out of sight.

The teams stood at stations set about thirty feet apart. Each station had the name of the team displayed on a post hammered into the ground. By each station were piles of logs and branches, lengths of rope and rolls of masking tape. It was mid-afternoon and a light breeze was blowing. The Percivals were all wearing wetsuits, but Voxy had said no to their offer of a *monster* wetsuit made out of plastic bin bags.

'Right,' said Mr Mills. 'For this event you will build a bridge from this side of the river to the other side.'

'Cool!' cried Voxy and Robbie.

'The bridge must be strong enough to carry everyone in your team across, *one at a time.*'

'Excellent!' shouted Kat.

'The river is only about four feet deep,' continued Mr Mills, 'but the current is very strong so every child will be expected to wear a lifejacket at all times.'

'I won't need one,' whispered Voxy. 'You saw how I pulled that boat into the harbour!'

'You may stand in the river when building your bridge,' went on Mr Mills, 'but for the final crossing, no part of you can be in contact with the water. Is that understood?'

'YES!' nodded everyone, eager to get on with the challenge.

Mr Mills checked his watch. 'And the time to begin,' he declared, 'is NOW!'

'OK,' said Robbie, as he and Kat pulled on their lifejackets. 'I think the best bridge design is to make "X" shapes out of logs and branches.

These can be supported by upright logs placed on the bed of the river.'

'Good idea,' said Robbie's dad, 'remember to think BIG! We can win this event!'

Voxy used his tail to chop the first two logs down to the right size. Robbie and Kat lashed them with the rope into an X shape while Robbie's parents waded into the river to dig in the first upright log. When everyone was ready, Voxy lifted the X over the water's edge to Mr and Mrs Percival, who received it and tied it their upright log.

'Try it out, Kat!' commanded Robbie.

Kat took a few tentative steps on to the X. It held firm, so she carried on to the end of it.

'It works!' cried Voxy.

When the second X was complete, Robbie carried it over the first X and tied the two Xs together with rope, while his parents secured the second upright log. He then hurried back to the bank. He and Voxy took a quick glance up the

168

river. Most teams hadn't got much further than the planning stage. The Carltons, however, had made a good start and their ladder-style bridge was about the same distance over the river as the Percivals'.

The Percival team worked fast, their Xs reaching the middle of the river in half an hour. Mr Carlton and Ian were working like crazy, and their bridge was neck and neck with the Percivals'.

Fifteen minutes later, Robbie tied the last X to the final log his parents had just hammered into the riverbed. The X touched the opposite bank – the Percivals' bridge was complete!

The Carltons were also just putting the finishing touches to their bridge.

Robbie had already crossed the bridge to the other bank so he stayed put. Kat quickly followed him across. Then Mr and Mrs Percival speed-waded out of the water and successfully made it across the brand new structure.

Mr Carlton had just made his way across the Carltons' bridge.

'COME ON, VOXY!' yelled the Percivals. Voxy stepped on to the bridge and started walking across. The bridge held firm. He looked over at the Carltons' bridge. Ian was crossing it – he was exactly parallel with Voxy.

I HAVE to beat that Carlton kid, whatever happens!

Voxy sped up and edged ahead of Ian, but as he stepped on to the last X, there was a loud cracking noise and the X snapped in two. Voxy wobbled for a second and then went crashing down into the fast-flowing water, landing with a colossal splash on his back.

'NOOOOO!' shouted Robbie, as the current dragged his monster friend downriver.

'SWIM TO THE SIDE!' called Kat.

'I CAN'T SWIM ON MY BACK!' shouted Voxy, trying without success to turn on to his front.

'YOU HAVE TO FLIP OVER!' yelled

Robbie, dashing down the bank, desperately trying to keep up with Voxy.

'I'M TOO HEAVY!' shouted Voxy, trying again in vain to twist over.

Robbie was running at full speed, but a few seconds later, the current sped up. Voxy crashed round the bend in the river and disappeared from sight.

Robbie raced round the bend. A short distance ahead he spotted Voxy, lying on his back, tangled up in some reeds. His body was completely still, and his eyes were closed.

'NO!' screamed Robbie, diving into the rushing water and swimming frantically towards Voxy. When he reached him, he put his ear against the monster's chest.

'What are you doing?' asked Voxy, opening one eye.

'YOU'RE ALIVE!' yelled Robbie.

'Of course I'm alive,' replied Voxy. 'I was just having a little snooze.'

*

'The Carltons were the first to finish and cross their bridge,' said Robbie's mum, when Voxy and Robbie re-joined the rest of their team. Voxy felt bad because it was him who'd broken the Percivals' bridge.

'It could have been any of us,' said Kat.

'Exactly,' nodded Mrs Percival.

'And anyway,' said Robbie, 'I bet the Carltons cheated!'

'You can't say that unless you have proof,' tutted Mr Percival.

When they got back to the site Mrs Percival ordered Robbie and Voxy to go and have a long hot shower and put some clean clothes on. It was dark by the time they came back from the washroom and they found a piece of paper stuck to the front of their tent.

DEAR R & V

THE NEXT EVENT IS STARTING
EARLIER THAN PLANNED SO WE'VE
HAD TO GO. IT'S TAKING PLACE DEEP IN
THE FOREST. MR MILLS WON'T TELL
US WHAT IT IS UNTIL WE REACH OUR
DESTINATION. WE HAVE LEFT A TRAIL OF
STONES SO THAT YOU CAN FOLLOW US
EASILY. HOPE YOU'RE BOTH NICE AND
DRY! GET TO US AS QUICKLY AS YOU CAN.

MUM, DAD & KAT

Robbie nipped inside the tent and grabbed a couple of torches. Voxy spotted an unopened packet of bread rolls and gobbled eleven, leaving one for Robbbie, which was plenty. They had just set off when a figure crossed their path.

'Farmer Millet!' said Robbie.

Farmer Millet owned the farm a couple of fields away. The Percivals had got to know him well over the years. He was tall and bearded, with large rosy cheeks.

'Hello, Robbie, nice to see you!'

'This is my friend Voxy,' said Robbie.

The farmer looked up at the huge creature. 'I could do with a sheep-monster,' he smiled, 'you'd really keep my sheep in order!'

Voxy and Robbie laughed.

'How's the Challenge going?' asked the farmer.

'OK,' replied Voxy, 'but we think one team is up to no good.'

Farmer Millet frowned. 'Well, I've hardly seen any of the events this year, apart from the axe one.'

Voxy and Robbie looked at each other. 'What axe event?' asked Voxy.

Farmer Millet explained and when he'd finished, Voxy and Robbie were very, very angry – but not with him.

'Thanks, Farmer Millet,' said Robbie. 'It's been very useful talking to you, but we have to go now!'

They ran off, following the trail of stones that had been left for them. This led them deep into the forest. They hadn't gone far when it started to drizzle.

And then the stone trail suddenly stopped.

'GOT LOST?' shouted a voice in the distance. Robbie held up his torch. Its pale light picked out Ian Carlton. He had a large pile of stones in his hands.

'HE'S TAKEN THE TRAIL!' cried Voxy. *I am going to sort out that Ian Carlton!*

But Ian dipped behind a tree and disappeared.

'How are we going to find them now?' asked Robbie, as the rain started to fall more heavily.

'Hang on,' said Voxy, cupping one of his wafer-thin ears and listening very carefully for a few seconds. 'I can hear your mum and dad arguing about some instructions,' he said. 'They're over there somewhere!' He pointed with his snout.

'Voxy – you're brilliant!' shouted Robbie, running on ahead.

Ten minutes later, Robbie burst into a clearing. His parents and sister were in the middle, busy working on the next event – making a waterproof shelter. They'd created a wigwam structure, leaning lots of logs against the base of a large tree.

'So glad you're here!' shouted Kat. 'Mum and Dad are arguing about the best way to build the shelter.'

'Where's Voxy?' asked Robbie's mum.

'He's right behind me,' said Robbie.

But when he turned round Voxy wasn't there.

Robbie peered back into the darkness. He took several steps in the direction he'd come from. He shone his torch in big swooping arches. He walked round the outside of the clearing. But there was no sign of the Zorb monster.

'VOXY!' Robbie shouted into the darkness. 'VOXXXXXYYYYYYYY!!'

'I'm sure he'll be fine,' said Mrs Percival, putting an arm round her son's shoulders.

'I'm going to look for him,' said Robbie.

'No,' said his dad. 'We don't want you getting lost. Voxy will find us. He's an incredibly clever monster.'

Robbie thought about this for a few moments. He was worried, but decided that Voxy would probably be OK. 'All right,' he sighed, 'what do you want me to do for the shelter?'

'We've made the basic shape,' explained his mum, 'and we've left a special high entrance so Voxy can get in. Kat is weaving branches in and out of the logs to make the shelter stronger. Why don't you make the top part more secure?'

'Definitely!' nodded Mr Percival. 'Remember to think BIG!'

Robbie tried hard to lose himself in this roof-strengthening task, but his mind kept switching back to Voxy. Where was he?

As the Percivals worked on, the rain started falling faster and more heavily. Soon, they were drenched, but they carried on, twisting, shoving, looping and weaving.

'KEEP GOING!' shouted Mr Percival above the din of the ferocious rain.

Thunder rumbled, followed by several silvery streaks of lightning in the sky.

'WE'RE FINISHED!' shouted Mr Percival, tying up a final twig.

'LET'S GO INSIDE!' shouted Kat, desperate to escape the downpour.

But just as they were about to step inside, a massive gush of rain cascaded down on to the branches and twigs and smashed the entire shelter to pieces.

DISASTER!

shrieked Kat.

But the collapsing shelter was nothing compared to what happened next.

A huge creaking noise sounded above the Percivals. They looked up and in horror saw six enormous tree trunks smashing down, straight towards them. They were about to be well and truly crushed!

9

A split second before the tree trunks hit the Percivals, they knitted together and made a huge A-frame around the tree the Percivals had been working on.

'You kept saying think BIG, Mr Percival!' cried Voxy, appearing out of the shadows.

'VOXY!' yelled Robbie, running over and giving him a huge high-five.

'I spied on the Carltons' shelter,' explained Voxy, the rain lashing down around him. 'I knew ours had to be better than theirs so I thought BIG and grabbed these trees! There

182

are thousands in the forest so I don't think six uprooted ones will make much difference.'

'That's great,' said Kat, checking her watch, 'but the challenge finishes in five minutes. We don't have enough time to make the shelter waterproof.'

'Oh yes, we do!' cried Voxy, as the rain poured down all around them.

These humans are in for a bit of seriously HARD work!

In lightning-quick movements, he used his tail to grab colossal amounts of branches, twigs and leaves off the forest floor. He stuffed these into the Percivals' arms. Next he grabbed Mr and Mrs Percival with his ears and Robbie and Kat with his tail.

'GET READY!' he cried.

He then started running round the outside of the shelter. As the Percivals whizzed past the structure they wove the branches and leaves between the six giant tree trunks.

'THIS IS BRILLIANT!' shouted Robbie.

Mr and Mrs Percival and Kat had all gone green in the face again, but they stuck to their jobs. By the time Mr Mills' booming voice declared the event was over and his inspection would soon begin, the Percivals' shelter was tightly packed and fully waterproof, with a tall bark front door that was able to open and close.

'EVERYONE INSIDE!' commanded Voxy. They ran in and slammed the door shut. The rain beat down on the outside of the shelter, but none of it got inside. All of the Percivals were shivering, so Voxy knotted his webbed toes together and they started to give off gusts of warm air.

'If you knot them when it's cold, they produce heat,' he explained, 'and if you do it when it's hot, they produce cool air.'

'How clever, Voxy!' smiled Mrs Percival. 'You never cease to amaze me!'

Voxy beamed proudly.

The lovely warm air made the shelter unbelievably cosy and delightfully comfortable. Voxy was just about to teach the Percivals some Melafon crowd chants when there was a tiny knocking sound on the front door. Voxy pulled it open a fraction. A small girl from the Sunderland family was standing outside, water pouring down on her. A few steps behind stood the rest of her drenched family.

'My name's Hannah,' she said, looking up at Voxy. 'Our shelter was knocked down by the rain.'

Voxy looked into her sad eyes and was silent for a few moments. Then a smile slowly spread over his face.

'Well, come inside, Hannah, and warm your bones!' he cried.

Hannah smiled a toothy grin, walked inside and gave Voxy a giant hug.

The rest of her family stood there in silence, not quite sure what to do.

'Er, hello, Sunderlands?' shouted Voxy. 'What's the point of getting even wetter when you can come in here and get warm and dry?'

Hannah's parents and younger brother walked slowly forwards and a few seconds later they were tucked inside the shelter.

'Thank you,' they all said, shooting guilty looks at Voxy.

'No problem,' grinned Voxy.

A minute later, there was another knock on the door. This time it was the Jobson family. Their shelter had collapsed too and they were also sopping wet. Voxy ushered them inside.

They were followed a few minutes later by the Ali family, then the Dentons, the Watkins and the Kahns. Voxy invited them all in. There was plenty of space and they all praised the wonderful cleverness of the roof structure.

'It only took Voxy five minutes to build it!' said Kat, 'with a tiny bit of help from us.'

'Impressive!' murmured several people.

Everyone also congratulated Voxy on his amazing knotted-toes heating system.

After quite a while, there was finally another knock on the door.

Voxy peered out.

It was the Carltons.

They were soaked to the skin and looking desperate. 'Sorry,' said Voxy, looking them up and down, 'we're full!' He slammed the door shut.

There was a great cheer inside the shelter.

Now that's what I call getting your own back! thought Voxy.

Half an hour later, the rain stopped, and Mr Mills came to check out all of the shelters. He soon discovered that the Percivals' was the only one standing.

'We'd better be getting back,' said someone, after Mr Mills had gone.

Before leaving, all of the other families thanked Voxy and the Percivals and then Voxy again. They patted him on the back and shook his claws.

At last it was just the four Percivals and Voxy remaining. They spent another twenty minutes chatting and laughing in the warmth of their shelter before finally making a move back to join the others.

When they reached the campsite they suddenly stopped. Their tents were now completely surrounded by all of the other tents on the site – all but one. On the far side of the field stood the Carltons' tent, alone and unloved.

'Look!' cried Kat.

There, hammered into the ground, was a sign.

DEAR VOXY

WE ARE ALL <u>SO</u> SORRY ABOUT
LISTENING TO MR CARLTON'S
INSTRUCTIONS ABOUT MOVING AWAY
FROM YOU SO THAT NEITHER WE NOR
OUR CHILDREN WOULD CATCH ANY DEADLY
DISEASES. YOU ARE A TRULY AMAZING
AND VERY MUCH UN-DISEASED MONSTER.
WE DON'T KNOW HOW WE CAN MAKE IT
UP TO YOU, BUT IF YOU WOULD LIKE, WE
WOULD ALL LOVE TO PLAY A GAME OF
MELAFON - IF THAT'S OK.

FROM EVERYONE ON THE CHALLENGE
(EXCEPT FOR THE CARLTONS)

Voxy's face lit up as people stuck their heads out of their tents and gave him smiles, waves and grateful bows. He was even more delighted, a few minutes later, when he passed the Carltons' tent and saw an open bin bag of rubbish beside it. On the off-chance that he might find something interesting, he had a quick rummage around and found a *fascinating* piece of paper: the till receipt from the Carltons' trip to Mrs Earnshaw's village store yesterday. He quickly headed back to Robbie to show it to him. No sooner had he done this than Mr Mills' voice rang out from his megaphone.

'Can everyone please go to the log circle!'

'This is it!' said Robbie, stuffing the receipt into his trouser pocket and heading to the circle with the rest of Team Percival. 'We *must* be in with a chance of winning the whole challenge. Our shelter was easily the best!'

This time at the log circle, it was the Carltons' turn to sit by themselves and the Percivals' turn to be surrounded by the other contestants. But this didn't seem to bother Ian Carlton and his father very much. They just sat there whispering to each other and sneering at everyone else.

'It is now time to declare which team are the winners of this year's challenge,' announced Mr Mills dramatically.

There were nervous looks and sharp intakes of breath around the circle.

'This year's overall winners,' declared Mr Mills, ' are … the Carltons!'

10

'IN YOUR FACE!' shouted Ian Carlton, running round the circle and shaking his fists triumphantly at everyone.

'YESSSS!' screamed Mr Carlton, leaping up, jiggling his body and laughing gleefully at the other contestants.

'Er … it's not quite over,' said Voxy, raising himself to his full height and fixing a beady eye on the Carltons.

'What do you mean, *not quite over?*' demanded Mr Carlton. He and his son stopped their celebrations.

'We have some very important information about the contest,' said Robbie.

'Surely you're not going to listen to these two idiots?' snapped Mr Carlton.

'I'd like to hear what they have to say,' said Mr Mills.

'US TOO!' shouted everyone else.

'Thank you,' said Robbie, 'Let's start with the bread-making event.'

'What about it?' snapped Ian. 'Our loaf was the best – end of story!'

'Voxy took rather a lot of photos earlier today,' said Robbie, holding up his camera, 'and one of them was this!'

He passed the camera round the circle.

'This photo is of the inside of the Carltons' car boot,' explained Voxy.

Everyone stared at the packet of fresh yeast, the large lump of shop-bought clay and the special bread flour, jutting out from beneath a grey blanket.

There were gasps round the circle.

I knew whizzing Robbie's camera around would come in useful! thought Voxy.

'The Carltons must have somehow worked out that bread-making would be one of this year's events,' said Robbie.

'So they brought all of this stuff to help them,' added Voxy.

'Do you have a photo showing us using any of that stuff *during* the bread-making event?' demanded Mr Carlton.

Robbie ignored him.

'Then, for the treasure hunt,' said Voxy, 'we couldn't work out what the bluey-white section on our map was, and why we ended up in a field full of angry bulls.'

'But Voxy found this receipt showing what the Carltons bought in the village shop yesterday,' said Robbie.

'And guess what?' chipped in Voxy, holding up the receipt. 'One of the things they bought was *a tube of bluey-white liquid paper*. The bluey-white section on our map was liquid paper. They used it to cover up a vital part of the map and sent us into a field of bulls!'

'YOU HAVE NO PROOF!' shouted Ian.

'We didn't actually *see* you changing our map,' said Robbie.

'But we did see Mr Carlton distracting Mr Mills, while Ian was in Mr Mills' tent altering it,' said Voxy. 'As soon as Ian appeared his father immediately lost all interest in his conversation with Mr Mills!'

'But you have no WITNESSES for any of your accusations!' yelled Mr Carlton.

'Oh yes they do,' said a voice from outside the circle.

Everyone looked up at once. Farmer Millet approached the circle.

'Thanks for joining us, Farmer Millet,' nodded Robbie. 'Would you mind telling us what you saw up by the River Rack earlier today?'

'I was walking along the bank,' explained the farmer, 'and I saw two people using an axe to chop at the underside of the logs at Team Percivals' station.'

'Are those people here?' asked Robbie.

'Yes,' nodded the farmer, pointing at the Carltons. 'It was those two.'

'Did they chop the logs *in half*?' asked Voxy.

'No,' replied the farmer, 'they were just making cuts in them, as if they were trying to weaken them in some way.'

'THERE YOU GO!' cried Robbie.

'They weakened our logs,' said Voxy, 'and that's why our bridge collapsed!'

For a few seconds no one spoke, but then the shouts started.

'OUTRAGEOUS!'

'DESPICABLE!'

'QUITE, QUITE HORRIBLE!'

Mr Mills stood up and raised his hands for silence.

The noise died down.

'I have never seen anything like this in all my years of organizing the Rackham Forest Camp-Out Challenge,' he said in a very grave voice. 'And as a result of everything that Voxy and Robbie have just told us, I hereby declare that the Carlton team are no longer the winners of this year's Challenge!'

There were loud cheers round the circle.

'NOOOOOOOOOO!' screamed Ian and his father in despair.

'If the Carltons hadn't cheated,' went on Mr Mills, 'I am sure the Percivals would have won the treasure hunt *and* the bridge building events. They also made the only shelter that stayed standing. Because of these factors, I now declare that this year's winners are ... the Percivals!'

There were screams, whistles and cheers. Team Percival stood up and took a modest bow.

'Now how about that game of Melafon?' shouted Voxy.

'YES!!!' yelled everyone.

What followed was a sensational Melafon game. Voxy captained one team, Mr Mills captained the other. Everyone got several turns at lobbing and flicking and many Fons were scored. The gamed finished well past midnight and ended 25 Fons each – a satisfactory result all round. Then everyone enjoyed a piping hot cup of cocoa and went over all of the weekend's events they'd taken part in. The atmosphere was joyous.

Mr Carlton and Ian sat a good distance away, under a dripping tree, muttering and hissing at each other.

Finally it was time for bed.

After saying loads of 'Goodnights', Voxy and Robbie finally climbed into their tent, very tired but very happy.

'Thanks to you, Voxy, we won this year's Camp-Out Challenge!' sighed Robbie sleepily.

'It was a team effort,' yawned Voxy, although he was secretly delighted about his role in defeating the Carltons and helping the Percivals to victory. He yawned and knotted his toes together, producing some deliciously warm jets of air. 'I reckon Mr Mills will ban the Carltons from ever entering again,' murmured Robbie.

'I reckon you're right,' replied Voxy softly.

A few moments later they were both asleep.

They were woken in the early hours of the following morning by the sound of two voices arguing, and the hammering in of tent pegs. They poked their heads outside and saw Mr Carlton and Ian re-pitching their tent as near to *theirs* as possible, and diving inside.

'I'm freezing,' groaned Ian, 'so I want to sleep nearest to Voxy's warm toe gusts.'

'I'm *more* freezing!' snapped his father, 'so *I* should be nearest!'

'Youngest gets the best spot,' whined Ian.

'Oldest gets first choice,' hissed Mr Carlton.

Voxy and Robbie closed their tent door and Voxy turned over so that the warmth from his toes blew in the opposite direction to the Carltons. It wasn't long before he and Robbie were both fast asleep again, but only after they'd had a very long, and a very hearty laugh.